One

"So, I've either got to find a new job or I've gotta find someone to marry me, ASAP," I said, sipping my Coke with lime. I wasn't much of a drinker, and since drinking out was hella expensive, I was soda-only and cheap beers at home on my couch.

As a result of a wacky grandmother, I had thousands of dollars in the bank with my name on them. One catch? I had to be married to collect. I'd lost my job last week, so I was flipping out about how I was going to support myself.

"I'd marry you," my best friend, Ansel, said as he grabbed a hot wing. "I mean, I don't have much to offer, and we'd definitely have to get an annulment, but I'd take a bullet for you, babe." I snorted into my soda.

"I don't think we could even be fake married." I loved him to the edge of the earth, but I swear, if we tried to even pretend to be a couple, we'd kill each other. Plus, there was the fact that he was gay and I wasn't into men.

"Yeah, probably a wise choice. I'm a pain in the ass," he said, sucking the sauce off his fingers.

"Must you do that?" I asked, handing him a napkin.

"You love me," he said, wiping off his sauce-covered face and hands.

"I do indeed," I said, sighing. "But seriously, what am I going to do?"

"I can see if we have any openings. Not sure if you're up for it, though."

"I'll think about it," I said to Ansel. He worked at a hospital, and I wasn't sure if I could handle that. I didn't know if I could deal with crying sick people and fighting with insurance companies.

"Seriously, do. Not every position is patient-focused. You could be happy as hell on a computer with your headphones on." That would be ideal. I wasn't super great at peopleing. Only a few of my jobs had been in customer service and I had quickly realized it was not in my wheelhouse, which cut out a lot of potential jobs.

"Or I could help you find someone to marry. I'm not sure how well I would do as a matchmaker, but I'd give it a shot." He was sweet, but I didn't need a matchmaker. The inheritance was a long shot. Most of the time I didn't even think about it.

"What possessed your grandmother to make that rule?" he asked me.

"I was three when she died, but I've heard stories. I guess she didn't like the fact that my parents weren't married when they had me. How dare!" I gasped and pretended to be scandalized.

"She sounds like a sassy lady." I laughed.

"Oh, she was. I've heard tons of stories. One time, a guy tried to grope her and she beat him with her umbrella until he ended up in the hospital. She could also make a killer cheesecake."

Ansel nodded.

"Both important."

"Agreed."

Coming out tonight with Ansel had been a good decision. My first inclination had been to stay home and wallow in my room with a lot of cake and potato chips. I hadn't ruled that out yet. I could do a lot in one night.

We finished our wings and sodas and he put his arm around me.

"You'll land on your feet, I promise. And if you need a few bucks to get you through, I'm here. I'm always here. I don't have much, but I'm here for you." I hugged him back and tried to hold back tears.

"You're a good friend, Ansel," I said, my voice a little shaky.

"So are you. You've been there for me, Lo, when a lot of people weren't." His eyes were misty too. He'd started transitioning two years ago, and some of the people we'd been friends with hadn't taken it well. I'd been struggling with figuring out my sexuality, so the two of us had sort of stuck together and had gone out on our own to find a new group who would appreciate us for how awesome we were, and we had.

I kissed him on the cheek and he mussed my hair.

"You're gonna be fine, Lo. Or, you might have to reactivate your online dating profile and make a few changes." I cringed. I'd attempted online dating when I'd first come out, hadn't had any success, and had found a lot of creeps and people who just weren't right for me. I didn't have much hope now.

"Keep your fingers crossed I find a job instead."

He held up his hands and crossed all his fingers except for his thumbs and then crossed his eyes at me.

"You got it."

I hadn't told my mom about losing my job yet, and the lying was killing me. We were pretty close, and I told her just about anything. But I couldn't tell her about this, because then she would try to give me money that she and Dad didn't have. Of course, he'd gotten money when Gram died, but all of it was gone now. Gone into the several-hundred-year-old farmhouse they lived in, and to medical bills when my mom had had her gallbladder out.

To add insult to injury, my car needed a bunch of repairs and wasn't drivable, and my rent wasn't exactly cheap. Living in Boston cost major bucks, but I wouldn't want to live anywhere else. I'd grown up just west of Boston, and had always set the city in my mind as where I eventually wanted to be. I went to BU and graduated with a degree in business and communications. I was a Boston girl, through and through.

I had more than a few friends that had made their way from small towns to Boston and had had to go back and live with their parents. I knew there was nothing wrong with that, but I couldn't handle the idea of that for myself. There wasn't a whole lot in the way of industry in my hometown. I couldn't go back.

My roommate, Lisa, was out when I got back. She and I weren't exactly friends, but we got along okay for two strangers who shared an apartment. We stayed out of each other's way, and it worked.

I grabbed a fresh bag of chips with pink sea salt and mixed up a quick mug cake to satisfy my need for something sweet. I stripped down to my bra and undies and put on one of my comfort romantic comedies.

"Thanks, Gram," I said, raising a chip to the ceiling. As a result of the whole "you have to be married to get the money," I wasn't really keen on the whole marriage idea. My parents had eventually gotten married when I was older, but only so they could share health insurance and file a joint tax return. They'd gone to the courthouse and told me about it after. There weren't even any pictures.

I guess I just didn't see the point. Why did you need to do something like that to prove your love? And don't even get me started about the wedding industry. Total expensive bullshit that somehow everyone thought was necessary. Hard pass.

No, I wasn't getting married. Fake or real.

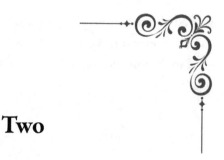

Two

I spent the next week chasing down job leads and eating a ton of peanut butter sandwiches, because I was trying to save as much money as possible. I'd also put some of my furniture and books up for sale online. Any little bit of cash was welcome.

Friday afternoon I got a text from Cara and, reading between the lines, something was up. I hoped she wasn't going to ask me for dating advice. I knew fuck all about dating men. We hadn't talked a lot lately since she'd been busy applying to grad school, and I missed her. I'd known Cara practically my whole life. Our desks had been put together in kindergarten and that had been it. We'd had a hiatus for a while when she'd moved across the country during high school, but she'd come back to Boston for college and we'd been just as close ever since.

Wanna get brunch tomorrow? I asked her.

Yes, please. Our usual place?

You got it.

I already knew what she was going to order. Blueberry pancakes, hash, and a glass of cranberry juice. She probably knew what I was going to order, even if I didn't yet. There wasn't a whole lot about Cara that I didn't know, and that was so comforting. I didn't want to burden her with my bullshit if she had her own, but it might come spilling out anyway. I could never keep a secret from her for long.

I WAS A FEW MINUTES late meeting Cara, and I rushed into the diner to find her already sitting at a tiny two-person table in the back. The place was packed, but that wasn't unusual. I smiled and squeezed through booths and tables and people to get to her.

"Hey, how's it going?" I asked, as she stood up to give me a hug. I closed my eyes and realized she was using a new perfume.

"Good, how are you?" she replied, and released me. I was about to ask about the perfume, but the look on her face made me forget about it.

"Uh, fine. Are you sure you're okay?" We both sat down and she looked away and I thought she was going to cry.

"Um, not really. I got into grad school," she said with a weak smile. "But they won't give me enough financial aide, and you know how my parents are, and so I can't go. I'm just having a hard time accepting it, I guess." Her chin wobbled and one tear rolled down her cheek.

"Oh, Cara, I'm so sorry. Come here," I got up to give her another hug just as our waitress came over to take our drink orders and tell us about the specials.

"Can you give us a minute?" I said, but Cara waved me off and sat back down.

"No, I'm fine." She wiped her eyes and ran her fingers through her light brown hair.

I couldn't think about ordering drinks, so I just got some tea and focused back on Cara.

"You can't work and go to school?" She shook her head.

"They told us not to. Plus, I'm going to need to do clinicals, and that's going to be unpaid." Of course. It was no wonder our generation was broke as hell.

"Did you put in an appeal?" I was trying to think of anything I could think of to fix this.

"Yeah, I've tried everything. Unless I can pull like twenty grand out of my ass, I'm screwed." Holy shit, that was a lot of money. "And that's just for the first year." She laughed a little and looked up at the ceiling, as if money was going to rain down on her.

"So there goes that dream. I don't get to be a physician's assistant after all. I can just go back to nursing, but..." she trailed off and wiped a few more tears. "It's just hard. To give up on that."

I could practically hear her heart shattering, and mine was breaking for her. I reached out and took her hand, squeezing it.

"We'll figure something out, Cara. You're not the only one who, uh, needs cash." I definitely didn't need that much, but I needed more than a few hundred dollars.

"I'm so sorry, I've been completely self-centered, what's going on with you?" I shouldn't have said anything. It wasn't a competition.

"I just kinda lost my job. So I'm looking for another one and rent is due and I have a little bit of savings, but not enough to get me through if it takes a few months. So, I guess we're both kinda fucked." I raised my cup of tea and she raised her glass of cranberry juice.

"Here's to being broke," she said, and a little bit of the mood lightened. It was a huge relief to see her smile, and for it to be genuine.

"You can always get a job at the hospital with me and Ansel." I added some more honey to my tea.

"Yeah, he already suggested that, but you know how I am with people. I swear, someone would come in with an injury and I'd either cry or throw up. I can't do blood." I shuddered at the thought.

"I know. One of us just needs to win the lottery. If I won, I'd give you what you needed." I knew she would. And so would I.

"If only my grandmother hadn't put that freaking clause on my inheritance. That would be more than enough to cover school for you and get me through a while without a job. I could make it stretch for years if I needed to. Ha, maybe we should get married." The second the words were out of my mouth, everything made sense.

"Cara, we can get married." Her brown eyes went as wide as I'd ever seen them go and her eyebrows almost disappeared into her hairline.

"We can *what*?!" She said it so loud that a few people turned and stared. I waited for them to go back to their French toast and hash browns.

"No, seriously, there's no stipulation on whether we have to be in love or anything. Just have a marriage certificate. We could get it annulled right afterwards. It would be so easy. I don't know why I didn't think of this before, it's brilliant." I reached out and grabbed her hand as our waitress came back to take our orders. I didn't want to be a bitch, but Cara and I had more important things to discuss right now.

I ordered pancakes and hash browns and ignored the waitress as she took our menus.

"Cara, this could work." Why wasn't she jumping up and down?

"No, Lo. I can't take that money from you. It's too much. And I wouldn't feel right about it. I know you don't care about marriage, but I do, and I wouldn't want to do it for the wrong reasons, and money isn't a good enough reason." I burst out laughing.

"Do you know how many marriages have started because of money? And how many marriages started between two people who didn't even like each other?" Rich people did that shit all the time. Hell, royals had done it for thousands of years. Why did we have to be any different?

"No, Lo. I can't do it." She shook her head and crossed her arms, as if to make it final.

I sighed.

"It would solve all of our problems, Care. It would take less than a week and we could have the money in our hands. And you could fulfill your dream and I could pay my rent and fix my car and stress a little less about finding a job. Don't forget, I need this money too. You'd be helping me get at it, and I'd be helping you in the process. It's perfect."

She frowned.

"I hadn't thought about it that way. I mean, you know that I would do anything for you, Lo, but..." she trailed off. "I just don't know if I can do that."

She sipped her cranberry juice slowly, and I gulped down my tea. I was high on the energy of my brilliant idea.

"You don't have to decide now," I said, even though I wanted her to say yes and agree and for us to make plans to go to the courthouse right away.

"Okay," she said. "I will think about it. I promise. It's just a huge surprise and a shock."

It wasn't every day that someone said "hey, let's get married so you can pay for grad school," but here I was with a solution to our dilemmas and I wanted nothing more than to share that money with her. There was more than enough for both of us. I knew my parents would support my idea of sharing the money with Cara. They loved her as if she was their own daughter, which was good, because her parents were the worst. I was glad she had finally cut off all contact with them.

Our food arrived and a silence descended on the table, but it wasn't uncomfortable. Cara and I had spent so many years together, silence wasn't a bad thing. My pancakes were perfect and fluffy as usual, but it didn't matter. I was itchy and wanted to leave. Whenever I got a good idea like that, I had to see it through immediately or else I couldn't sit still. I wanted action, now. Cara had never been like that. She was the kind of person who looked at every single angle and made countless lists and took forever to decide. Maybe that was good, since she was in the medical field and people's lives were in her hands. I couldn't even imagine. I was much more happy with computer data that wouldn't die if I made a mistake.

"Got any good stories for me?" I asked. Cara always had interesting stories from the hospital, and sometimes they were about her coworkers.

"Two of the EMTs got caught banging in an ambulance they were supposed to be restocking. Of course they just got reprimanded, but I can't even imagine the looks on their faces when they got caught." We both laughed.

"That's some Grey's Anatomy shit right there." She rolled her eyes.

"I hate that show."

"I know you do," I said. Cara had a problem with almost any medical drama because they got everything wrong, and she spent most of her time yelling at the screen. It was adorable and sometimes I wanted to watch things with her just to see it.

She told me some more stories, but in the back of my mind, I was only thinking about the money. And about putting a hypothetical ring on Cara's finger.

Three

Of course I couldn't keep my mouth shut and I told Ansel about my idea when we had pizza on Sunday night. He'd agreed to buy, and threw in a pitcher of cheap beer that I was slowly sipping, along with water.

"That would make way more sense than you and I getting married. Especially since you both need money." Cara wasn't any more attracted to me than Ansel was, and she'd been my best friend since we were kids. There weren't any kind of romantic feelings involved, so it would still be a marriage for the money.

"I know. She's hesitant about it, and I get that, but we both need this, and I know if she was in the same boat, she'd do the same. And I'm sure she'll try to do some sort of ridiculous repayment plan or something. God, she's probably working one out right now, with interest." That was probably exactly what she was doing right now. I could see her with her brows furrowed in concentration.

Ansel chuckled.

"You're right. I'm sure she is." Obviously Ansel hadn't known Cara as long as I had, but they'd met at the hospital right around the time I'd met him at a queer event, and had grown close in the years since.

"It just frustrates me that there's a solution to a problem, and she might not want to do it. I just don't want her to give up on her dream. She's been wanting this her whole life. She used to operate on my stuffed animals and take out their fluff organs and then try to sew them back up."

Ansel snorted into his slice of pizza.

"Not gonna lie, that's a little disturbing."

"I used to hand her the knife my parents told me I wasn't ever supposed to touch, so there you go." He raised his eyebrows.

"Now I'm scared of both of you."

"You should be," I said, tipping my beer at him.

I WAS GOING BERSERK waiting to hear from Cara. I had to fight every single urge in my body to text her and ask her what she thought. Instead, I texted and asked how she was.

Not great. Still crying.

Oh, that was not gonna fly. I asked her if she was at home and she said she was. Since I didn't have a job anymore, I could do things like go and rescue one of my best friends in her moment of need in the middle of the day. I also brought cannoli from Mike's Pastry, and a freshly made green juice with turmeric. I figured they were both needed.

I didn't let her know I was coming over until I was outside her door.

Are you serious was the only response when I texted that I was waiting for her to let me in.

A few moments later, there she was, unlocking the door and letting me in with a shake of her head.

"You're ridiculous."

"I know. But you love it," I said, holding out the box of cannoli and the green juice.

"I do, and thank you." Her eyes were red and puffy, and her cheeks were ruddy from streaking tears.

We walked up a set of narrow stairs to her tiny apartment at the top floor of the house, and settled down in her microscopic living room. There wasn't even room for a full-size couch, only a love seat and a tufted chair perpendicular to it.

I decided to suck down the green juice and chase that with a cannoli. Cara went right for the cannoli.

"I needed this so much," she said through a mouthful.

"I wish you'd called me sooner. I would have been here. I can be here now because I don't have a job. Yay." I waved my hands in mock excitement.

"Have you had any luck so far?"

"Not really. I've gotten a few immediate rejections, and no interviews yet. I don't expect to hear on some for at least a week or more. Finding a job takes time. I wish one of those headhunters would find and recruit me. How do you get head hunted?"

She finished her first cannoli and licked her fingers.

"I have no idea. But if anyone should get head hunted, it should be you." I squeezed her shoulder.

"Aw, thanks."

There was a lull as I selected my first cannoli and Cara grabbed her second. I wasn't quite sure how to bring up what I really wanted to know. As if she was reading my mind, Cara said, "So I thought about it. The marriage thing."

"And?" I said, nearly jumping off the chair and dropping my cannoli.

"And... I'm still on the fence. It just seems like such a bad idea, Lo. Like, I'm afraid god is going to strike us down if we do this. Or that the government will put us in jail."

"I mean, if we'd tried to get married a few years ago, we wouldn't have been able to, but it's all legal and shit now. The government, and god, have bigger things to worry about than if we're getting married for love or money. And, to be fair, I do love you. You're my best friend, Cara. Always have been. Don't tell Ansel." He would be extremely upset if he knew I'd called Cara my first and most best friend.

She smiled softly.

"I will. But I'm not sure."

"What can I do to convince you?" I would do literally anything, including singing karaoke, which was my greatest fear.

"I don't know, Lo." Cara set her cannoli down and put her head in her hands. "It's just... who does that? Who has a marriage of convenience?" Oh, was that what we were calling it? I kind of liked the sound of that. Even if being married to Cara would be a little more than convenient.

"People have been doing what we're doing since the dawn of time. I can print you out a list if you want. But it's gonna be a damn long list. We're not doing anything wrong. That money is just sitting there, waiting to be used. It *wants* to be used. 'Spend me, please!' it says." That made her laugh, and I felt like I was getting through to her.

"Are you sure you want to give it to me? I mean, I'll pay you back. I promise. I have a payment plan." She jumped up and grabbed a folder from her desk that sat in the corner of the room under the eaves.

"I knew we wouldn't get through this without a spreadsheet," I said. Cara was just so cute and predictable.

"I mean, it's just a general idea," she said, handing it to me. I barely looked it over, but I pretended to scan it.

"This looks good. But you don't have to pay me back. It's only if you want to, and if you have the money." If she could get through school, she would make decent money as a PA. Much more than I could ever hope to make with my current career trajectory. Maybe I should go back to school. Everyone in Boston seemed to have at least a Master's. I was always surrounded by so many educated people.

"I will pay you back. That's non-negotiable. With interest." I wanted to protest the interest, but I would agree to anything if only she would say yes.

"Okay," I said, and she inhaled deeply.

"Okay, then. Let's do this."

I jumped up.

"Are you serious?" I wanted to tackle-hug her.

"Yes. Hell, I'm going to regret this later, but right now I want to do this so you don't have to worry. Me getting the money is secondary." Of course it was. I'd feel the say way, in her shoes.

"So, we're getting married?" I needed confirmation.

"We're getting married?" It sounded like a question.

"Oh, we can't do it like this. Come on." I grabbed her hand and started dragging her toward the front door.

"Where are we going?" she said, stumbling along behind me. It didn't hurt that I was a few inches taller and she was a little bit clumsy.

"Rings. We need rings, obviously. And I'm not turning down this opportunity to propose. Don't worry, I won't do it in public." I let her gather her stuff and I grabbed my bag before we dashed to the closest train station and I looked up a cheap but nice jewelry store.

"We don't have to do this," Cara said at least five times before I dragged her into the store.

"Where are your lab-created stones? We need two rings," I said to the woman standing behind the lighted cases. She blinked a few times at me and then looked at Cara, who was red-faced.

"They're right over here," she said, gesturing to the back of the store. All the expensive shit was front and center.

"Are these for a special occasion? Are you sisters? Friends?" I opened my mouth to correct her, but Cara spoke first.

"Friendship rings," she said, stepping on my foot just enough to get her point across. Was she having an issue that this woman would think we were a real couple? Or was she still worried about the whole "marriage" part of what we were doing?

"Very nice," the woman said, visibly relaxing. I wanted to roll my eyes at her, but a look from Cara stopped me. She was going along with my plan, so the least I could do was make things easy on her.

"So these are the rings we have. Not sure what you're looking for." I was struck immediately by a ring with a round emerald with cubic zirconia on either side. It was pretty and green and simple. Perfect.

"That one," I said, pointing to it. That was the ring I wanted. The price was right and then it was up to Cara.

"I don't know," she said, biting her lip. I knew she wanted to do a pro and con list, and compare prices, but if we did that, we'd be in here for days.

"What about that one?" I asked, pointing at a rose gold ring that had one single oval opal set on the top. It was beautiful and sweet. Perfect for Cara.

"Can I try it on?" she asked, her voice barely above a whisper. I could tell already that she liked it by the way her hand shook as the saleswoman slid it on her finger.

"It's a perfect fit," she said. "That means it's the right one. It was waiting for you." Cara turned her hand right and left. The saleswoman had put it on her right ring finger instead of the left. My ring was too big, so she had to get one from the back. I quickly slipped the too large one on my left finger. Why did it make such a difference? Now I was the one with shaking hands.

"Are you sure we're doing this?" Cara whispered as the saleswoman came back with the right size ring for me.

"Is there anything else I can do for you today?" she asked and we both shook our heads.

"Nope, this is it," I said. She quickly rang us up, seeing that we weren't going to be giving her a huge commission, and got us out the door.

"Holy shit," Cara said, holding up the bag with the ring box inside.

"Yeah, holy shit. We've got rings, now all we need is a proposal and then a marriage certificate. Then we can live our dreams, corny as that sounds. Thank you so much for agreeing to do this, Cara. I can't imagine fake marrying anyone else." There was a lump in my throat for some reason. I had no idea why I was getting so emotional. Maybe it was the idea of seeing that opal ring on her finger and knowing that I was the reason it was there. And I'd have my own ring as well.

"What are you going to tell your parents?" she said.

I started laughing.

"I have no idea. I hadn't thought that far ahead." Why hadn't I considered that people were going to know about this marriage?

"I think we should tell them the truth. Plus, they're going to know. But as far as other people, I don't really want to be the girl who has the fake marriage for money. So..." she trailed off.

"So, what are you saying?" My stomach dipped as if I was on a roller coaster.

"I'm saying that we're gonna have to fake it. At least for a little while. I'm not saying we have to have a big declaration or anything, but I'm going to tell people I'm married. That we'd been friends for a long time and it turned into something more and we just decided one day to do it. Not that far from the truth, is it?" No, it wasn't. My stomach rolled again, and it was hard to breathe. What was happening to me?

"Yeah, you're right. We'll tell people we're married. Only the closest will know why we're doing it. Everyone else will get the story." Cara nodded.

"Okay. That makes me feel better. But before we announce anything, I think we should come up with a story. Because people are going to ask." This was why I needed her in my life. She thought of things I would never consider.

"Yeah, that's cool. Do you want to go back to your place?"

"Sure. I need a few more cannoli to deal with the fact that I have an engagement ring." She held up the bag again and I snatched it from her.

"No you don't." I handed her mine. "You don't get to have your ring until I propose. And vice versa." She blinked at me a few times.

"What have I gotten myself into with you, Loren?" I loved it when she called me by my full name, I didn't know why.

"Only one way to find out," I said in a singsong voice as I started walking down the sidewalk.

Four

My intention was to propose to Cara as soon as we got back, but for some reason I couldn't. It wasn't a big deal, I just had to hand her the ring and say the words, but I kept looking for an opening and it didn't feel right. I couldn't find a good moment, so we spent the rest of the afternoon stuffing ourselves with cannoli and complaining about capitalism. The rings remained in their boxes in the corner of the room. I could feel them sitting there. Watching. Judging. How could two such tiny items cause so much pressure?

"Do you want to stay over?" she asked a few hours later. The cannoli were long gone and it was dinner time. I had been just about to suggest that we order pizza.

"You mean like old times? We won't get to sleep in the hayloft." She smiled and rolled her eyes.

"I will never forget that time you told me that story about the farmer using the barn as his murder shed and that the walls were painted with the victim's blood," she said.

"Yeah, maybe that wasn't the best story to tell before we went to sleep that night. Sorry about that?" Cara threw the empty cannoli box at me.

"Brat. But seriously, do you want to stay over? No murder stories this time." The idea of going back to my apartment and being alone in my room sounded miserable, so I agreed.

"Do you mind if I go back and just grab some things real quick?"

"Not at all. I'll go with you." That was sweet of her, but that was the kind of friend Cara was. I hadn't won the lottery when it came to money, but I'd won the friend lottery, that was for sure.

BY THE TIME WE GOT back to Cara's from going to my place, we were both hungry enough to eat our rings instead of wearing them. Cara ordered pizza and I put my cutest pajamas on. She dashed out of the room and then came back in a tank top with dancing avocados on it and a pair of matching green pants.

"Oh my god, you look adorable." I stood up and she did a little twirl.

"So you do. I love these." She tugged at my pants that had otters all over them, including lots of otter puns. I'd fallen in love with them online and hadn't been able to resist buying them.

I grabbed her hand and made her do a little turn under my arm. We both laughed. We'd done the same thing when we were kids after watching some old movies that had waltzing couples in them.

"How come you always get to lead?" she said, not letting go of my hand.

"Because I'm taller? I don't know. Isn't that how it works?" She shrugged and finally dropped my hand.

"I don't know about that."

We were interrupted by my phone ringing with my mother's ringtone.

"Hey, Mom."

"Hi, baby. How are you doing? I haven't heard from you in a while." That was true, I was a bad daughter sometimes and didn't call her as much as I should.

"I'm good. Listen, I'm at Cara's house. We're having a sleepover tonight, like old times."

"Oh, let me talk to her. I haven't talked to her in a long time either. You both need to be better about that." As far as my mom was concerned, she had two daughters instead of one. I was so glad Cara had someone who loved and cared for her as a mother.

"She's right here," I said, handing the phone over.

"Hey... Yeah, I know. I'm sorry, I know I should call more," Cara said, making a face at me. She was having the same conversation with Mom.

I crashed on the couch as Cara walked around the room and chatted with Mom. At one point, she pulled the phone away and whispered to me, "do you want to tell her?"

"Now is as good a time as any," I said.

"Hold on, I'm putting you on speaker."

"What are you two up to? I can only imagine," Mom said.

"Well, you know how Gram left me that money? Turns out we both kind of need it, so, uh, we're getting married. For the money. Because we're awful like that."

There was silence on the other end for a few seconds.

"Of course you are. Honestly, I'm not surprised at all. You should have thought of that sooner. Could have used some of it for your undergrad."

"I mean, it's a little late for that, but you're okay with this, right?" I glanced at Cara. She looked worried.

"Absolutely. You know that I didn't get along with her and she made my life hell. Did I tell you that she tried to break up your father and I more than a few times?" This was the first I was hearing of it.

"Uh, no? I didn't know about that. I want to hear about that later, though."

"She was a mean woman with a lot of money, and for some reason, she decided to give a lot of it to you. So take advantage. It's not like she's going to know or approve because she isn't here anymore." I could tell my mom was glad about that fact, even if she wouldn't say it out loud.

"You sure you're okay with it?" Cara asked, and I turned the phone toward her.

"You both know my thoughts on marriage. I don't really care about it, and you're going to get it annulled after you get the money, right?"

"Yeah," I said.

"Then what's the problem? It's like cosigning a loan. In fact, it's even less serious than that because you're on the hook for a loan even if you're not in contact with the other person anymore. Go for it, girls. But tell me more about why you need money."

I figured she was going to ask about that, so I took her off speaker and handed the phone back to Cara. She told Mom about her financial aid situation and then handed the phone to me to explain about losing my job. The pizza came as I was trying to get her off the phone.

"I wish your father was home so you could talk to him, so expect a call probably tomorrow." I cringed, but I'd expected that.

"Sounds good," I said. Sometimes I envied people who only talked to their parents once a month or less. At times it felt like mine were too involved for me being twenty-three.

After ten more minutes of trying to get her off the phone, I finally succeeded. Cara had set up her small card table with her best plates and filled two wine glasses with a mixture of seltzer water and juice.

"Wow, isn't this fancy," I said, putting my phone on silent. I didn't have any faith that my mom wouldn't call again tonight. She'd done it before.

"Why not?" she said.

"I don't know," I replied, sitting down and picking up my glass. She lifted hers and we clinked them.

"To our impending marriage," I said. The word left a strange taste on my tongue. It was so adult. So mature.

"To our impending *fake* marriage," Cara corrected.

"Right." I knew it wasn't the real deal. It wasn't like we were going to fall in love with each other or anything. I had literally never thought of Cara that way, and she was completely and totally heterosexual. Sure, she hadn't had a boyfriend in a while, but that didn't mean anything. Cara was the kind of girl who wouldn't accept less than she deserved when it came to relationships, and a lot of the guys she'd tried to date hadn't been able to handle that. Their loss.

I inhaled as much pizza as I could and then we smushed together on the loveseat and watched old TV shows until we were ready to pass out.

"So you can crash here, or we can share the bed," she said, and my stomach did something funny. Probably too much melted cheese.

"Yeah, I don't think I'd be comfortable out here." She was basically in my lap and I'd been absently running my fingers through her hair.

"That's fine. There's enough room for two," she said, getting up.

"Lucky for me," I said, stifling a yawn. This had been a wild week and I was pretty fucking exhausted. At least I'd solved a bunch of my problems. I didn't have to stress about finding a job, any job, right now. I could pick and choose and maybe find something that would pay better and would be a better fit for my resume. And Cara would be able to tell the financial aid office to fuck off, she'd gotten the money another way.

"You ready for bed?" she asked, and I levered myself off the couch.

"If I don't go now, I'm going to be too tired to go to bed later." She nodded and yawned wide.

"I know exactly what you mean."

It was comical trying to cram both of us in her microscopic bathroom to brush our teeth at the same time. We kept bumping each other with our hips and laughing. I almost choked on my toothpaste.

One thing that Cara hadn't compromised on was her bed. It took up nearly her entire bedroom and was made with silky gray sheets and a light-yellow comforter with black flowers on it. There were even enough pillows for two people.

"This is the nicest bed I've ever slept in, except maybe for a hotel once or twice."

Cara pulled down the comforter so we could get in and I slid between the sheets and blankets and sighed in relief.

"Why thank you. I spent way too much on this bed, but I figure a bed is a good investment. Sleep is really important." It was, and right now, I needed it desperately.

She got in next to me and turned on her side.

"Thanks for coming over. And for having this ridiculous idea. I know I was reluctant at first, but I'm on board now. I'm not going to lie, I'm a tiny bit excited to get proposed to, even if it isn't real. I wonder what my future husband is going to think about that when I tell him I was married before him." When she mentioned a future husband, a sharp pain went through my chest.

"If he does mind, then he's not the right guy for you." I could barely get the words out. I didn't want to talk about this.

"That's so far in the future. I'm not planning on getting married until I'm a least thirty. That still feels like it's so far away, even though it's only seven years." Her eyes drifted closed and she yawned again. I hoped she was falling asleep so we could stop having this conversation.

"Let's just get through the fake marriage first," I said, and she nodded.

"Goodnight," she said opening her eyes one more time. I was closest to the light, so I got up and turned it out before crawling back into bed with her. She'd scooted over so we were almost pressed against each other. The bed was big enough, but I didn't mind her being that close. We'd always cuddled when we were kids and had even shared sleeping bags dozens of times. I knew the sounds she made in her sleep. The little whimpers when she was having a dream, or the little sighs, or the tiny snores when her nose was a little bit stuffy.

I'd slept in the same space with Cara hundreds of times before. So why did it feel different tonight? I lay on my back, staring at the ceiling and wondering why I couldn't sleep. I was aware of every single breath Cara took, every single little movement she made. I could barely breathe myself, and I kept as still as I could so I didn't disturb her.

What was *wrong* with me? This had nothing to do with pizza.

I let my mind wander and gave up on sleep after a few hours. It finally latched on one thing: the proposal. I thought of at least a hundred different ways I could do it, but none were right. Why was I spending so much time on this? I didn't know, but I wanted it to be good. Even if it was fake. It would be good practice for the future, maybe. So far this fake marriage thing had been pretty good. Maybe the real thing wouldn't be so bad, either. Or maybe I was just being a huge dork and was wrong about everything. That was also a huge possibility.

At one point, Cara made a little grunt in her sleep and wiggled closer to me. I froze, worried if I moved, I would wake her up. She nuzzled right into my shoulder and sighed in her sleep.

Carefully, I turned a little so her head was tucked more fully into my body. She was warm, and it was a hot night, but I didn't care. I'd sweat my brains out before I would move.

Sighing myself, I let my face rest against the top of her head, and finally my body decided it was time to shut down.

Five

I didn't propose the next day. Or the next. I kept the ring with me at all times, even when I was in the shower. It was too small for my ring finger, so sometimes I put it on my pinky. I had no idea what Cara was doing with my ring, but neither of us had mentioned them, and the longer we went like that, the bigger the rings seemed to grow, until I finally just decided to do it.

"Why are you making such a big deal out of this? It's not like it's real. Or is it for you?" Ansel asked, when I'd complained to him about it. I figured I needed someone not involved with the situation to talk to about it. I'd considered some of my other friends, but Cara and I were closest to Ansel, so it made sense to burden him with both of our issues.

"No, it's not real, are you high? It's literally just for the money and just on paper. Cara has been my best friend forever. Friend. I don't think of her that way. Plus, she doesn't like girls. Remember?" Ansel smirked, as if he didn't believe me.

"What are you saying? That I'm secretly in love with her and I created this need for money so I can marry her and seduce her into falling in love with me? You're giving me way too much credit, dude." I wasn't some criminal mastermind from some movie. I was just a broke girl who had a broke friend who needed to marry her so they could be un-broke. Simple.

"I'm not *not* saying that," he said, and I briefly considered dumping my soda on his head.

"You're an asshole sometimes."

"Yes, you're finally getting it! Congratulations." Now I definitely wanted to dump soda on his head. I picked up my cup and he put his hands up.

"No, don't mess up my hair. It's doing this perfect swoosh thing today." I slowly set my soda down and narrowed my eyes. His hair was looking good today. It was a color in between brown and blonde, and he probably took longer to style it than I did with my entire morning routine. He worked hard, and it showed. I couldn't mess with Ansel's hair. That was a crime I couldn't commit.

"Fine. Your hair escapes a soda bath. Just for today. But I'm not ruling it out in the future."

"You mess with my hair and we are no longer friends, Lo." I waved him off.

"Fine, fine. Your hair is safe. Promise." He dramatically held out his pinky finger and I linked it with mine.

"So back to this thing you have going with Cara," he said, and I groaned.

"Leave it alone, Ansel. Just leave it alone."

He didn't, and pestered me for the next hour until I threatened to leave.

I couldn't make him believe that I wasn't doing this whole thing because I was somehow in love with Cara. How ridiculous was that? And even if I was, she was never gonna feel that way about me, so it didn't matter. Still, I couldn't figure out why Ansel's comments wouldn't stop bugging me. I was grumpy and irritated for the rest of the day. It was Saturday and Cara had stuff going on until the evening, and I was even grumpier and missing her. It was silly since I had seen her yesterday, and I was going to see her tonight. I looked down at my pinky every now and then at the ring. I should do this. I should do this and get it over with. I had built it up and that was making me more anxious and stressed.

I didn't want to make a massive deal out of it, but I also didn't want to hand it to her while we were sitting in her living room. What was the happy medium between a massive romantic proposal and shoving the ring at her? There had to be something.

The internet was my friend, so I took to Google to see what a nice, casual proposal would look like. After scrolling, I realized that all those proposals were for other people. I needed something that was for *us*.

After a long shower to think, that ended up being ice cold at the end, I finally had it.

I was gonna kill it at this proposal. Go big, or go home, right? No matter if it was real or fake.

"Okay, what are you doing, you weirdo?" Cara said when I showed up twenty minutes early for our outing at her house.

"Oh, nothing," I said, affecting an airy tone. I'd dressed up just a little bit, but not enough to make her suspicious. I hoped.

"I just never know with you, Loren," she said, smirking and leaning against the door. There was a little flutter in my chest about her using my full name.

"Damn right. Come on, put on something nice." I shifted the large tote bag I had on my shoulder. It wasn't a basket, but I wasn't hauling a damn basket all over Boston.

She raised her eyebrows, but went back to her bedroom and I set my bag down for a minute.

"How was Ansel?" she asked, as I waited in the kitchen for her. Her bedroom door was cracked just a little bit and I could see her naked back as she slid a dress over her head. I looked away.

"What?" I asked. I'd forgotten what she'd said.

"How was Ansel?" she repeated. I was using all my energy to not look at her as she slid on some wedges and walked out. It wasn't like I hadn't seen her naked before. What was my deal?

"Oh, he was his usual charming self." I wasn't going to tell her about him pestering me. I definitely didn't want to plant that seed in her head and take the chance that it would grow and she'd think I was doing this for anything other than the money.

"I haven't seen him in ages and I miss him. Maybe I'll see if he wants to get a drink next week." Her dress was floaty and made of a black fabric covered in bright tropical flowers. She looked like a goddess when she moved. I felt like an ogre in comparison, but that was how things went with Cara. I remember when we hit puberty that she just kept getting prettier and I just kept getting more awkward, and that hadn't changed with age. I could clean up as best I knew how, but she would always top me in the beauty department. There was no doubt about that.

"You should," I said, a belated reply.

"I think I'll text him right now," she said, getting on her phone. My nerves started to get the better of me. Was this a terrible idea? Was she going to think it was awful? Was she going to say no and change her mind? Was she going to think I was making too much of this?

I didn't know, and I wouldn't know until I did it. I'd started the ball rolling and I had to let it go and see what happened.

Fingers crossed.

Six

I refused to tell Cara where we were going, so I had to tell her when we had to get off the subway. I could see the wheels clicking in her mind, but she didn't know where we were going. She couldn't.

Once we got to the street, I pulled out my phone to make sure I knew where I was going and then said, "this way." She gave me a skeptical look before following. I'd brought us to one of the main shopping areas in the city, but I bypassed most of the big stores, and took her down a few side streets to some smaller shops.

"This one," I said, pointing to a small shop with an awning. Cara looked up at it and smiled.

"You would bring us to a candy place."

"I wouldn't be me if I didn't," I said, holding the door open for her. "This is just the first stop. I have some more adult stuff in mind." That made her raise her eyebrows.

"Not adult like *that*, Care. Get your mind out of the gutter." We walked together into the shop that looked like Willy Wonka's wet dream.

"Never," she said, nearly crashing into a display of candy bars. I grabbed her arm at the last second.

The place was cram-jammed full of every kind of sweet thing imaginable, floor to ceiling. I didn't even know where to look. Bins of jellybeans, buckets of salt water taffy, bouquets of flower-shaped lollipops. I went right for those and grabbed a basket to put the lollipops in.

"You're not getting those for me, are you?" she asked, lurking behind me, looking a bit more apprehensive.

"Yes, I am. You don't have to eat them all. Go ahead and get whatever you want." Her eyes lit up.

"Even coconut jelly beans?" she asked. I made a disgusted face.

"Yes, even those. Ew." She had the oddest taste in candy, but I couldn't help but laugh as she scampered through the shop, both of us filling up my basket pretty damn quickly. I made sure to get some of the stuff I liked as well, and then spent a small fortune at the checkout counter before I filled my tote bag.

Our next stop was a wine and cheese shop for something a little more grown up. I picked a bottle of sweet sparkling wine and Cara got a premade cheese plate with prosciutto, olives, and crackers.

After we had the food, I steered us in the direction of the river. I hoped we could find a semi-secluded spot so we could just sit together and I could do my thing.

It took a while, and I was about ready to dump the candy, which was beyond heavy, but at last we got a good spot where there weren't too many people and we had a great view of the city, as well as a clear patch of grass free of goose poop. I hoped.

"I should have brought a blanket. I didn't put that on the list," I said, sighing.

"You made a list? I'm so proud." Cara clapped her hands and I stuck my tongue out at her as I dumped the candy down with a thump.

"Now I wanted to take you to my parent's house and go up in the barn and maybe hang this damn thing from the ceiling and have you pluck it down, but you know that I'm not that organized. You are. So I'm expecting something spectacular. But you know me, so you probably knew this was how it was going to be." I couldn't not do the traditional thing and get on one knee, so I said that and held out the ring. She already knew what it looked like, so I didn't have to do the whole dramatic thing with the box.

Cara was still standing and I couldn't stop looking at her face. In that moment, there was nothing more real than the expression on her face. Her hands trembled as she held them up to her mouth. As if she was shocked. As if this was the real deal.

"You are such a dork," she said in a soft voice. "And you forgot the question."

Oh, right. I should have written this down, but my whole thing was going to be spontaneous.

"Cara Lynne Simms, will you marry me so we can both get at my grandmother's money?" She held out her hand and I slid the ring on her left hand.

"Yes, Loren Alyssa Bowman, I will marry you to get at your grandmother's money." I heard someone cheering and Cara went beet red. She immediately sat down and hid her face with her hands.

"You said this wasn't going to be in public," she said through her hands.

"I didn't think anyone was paying attention. No one in Boston is usually paying attention to anyone else." She let her hands drop and looked around to make sure no one was staring. No one was. They'd all gone back to their own business.

"Give me my candy," she said, holding her hands out.

"Fine, fine. I worked for like, an hour on this proposal. I mean, I wrote down a bunch of ideas that I scrapped and decided to do this instead, but still. I worked on this." Cara got the bag of coconut jelly beans open and crammed a few in her mouth and grinned at me.

"You did good. Now I have to do something better. I can't let you top me." I cringed at the jelly beans and pulled out a chocolate bar that had caramel and nuts in it.

"You don't have to propose. I didn't have to do it, but I figured I would, since we had the rings and all. No pressure. I need to contact the guy who is in charge of the account and let him know that I'm getting married so he better be working on getting me a check. I know he's going to want to see the marriage certificate, so we'll probably have to fax him a copy or something. But as soon as I have the check? Cha-ching!" I devoured the rest of the candy bar and went for the cheese and crackers.

"We should have a toast," Cara said, opening the wine. "Do you have any glasses?" Shit, I'd forgotten something else.

"I really needed you to help me plan this. I'm a mess without you." Cara took a swig from the wine bottle and passed it to me.

"We don't need cups, see?"

I smiled at her and sipped from the bottle. We could always make it work.

"No, we don't need cups. Here's not needing cups, and marrying for money." I raised the bottle and had a sip before passing it back to her.

"Here, here," she said before drinking from the bottle as well.

"This is really nice, Lo," she said, leaning back and grabbing some cheese. "You did a good job. And you didn't have to. We didn't need to do the rings. But I can't help but feel good that it's on my finger. It's so pretty." She held out her hand and tipped it back and forth to watch the shine.

"Now you're making me jealous." I looked down at my left hand that didn't have a ring on it.

"You'll get yours. Now that I know what's expected of me." I waved her off. I hoped she didn't do anything too outlandish. We just needed to get our asses to the courthouse and get this done. Honestly, I had no idea how to even get married. Could we just go and do it? I had no idea. I should probably figure that out ASAP.

"Can we just go and get married whenever, or do we have to do something else? People go to Vegas and do it, right?" She shook her head.

"No. I'm not sure about Massachusetts law, but we probably have to get a marriage license and then wait for a few days before we go to the courthouse." Damn. That sucked.

"Ugh. Well, we should do that next week, right?"

Cara nodded and looked at the grass.

"I know this is fake and everything, but..." She sighed and looked up at me.

"But what?" Panic had struck me like a speeding train.

"But I kind of want to... do it. Like, have a pretty dress and a bouquet. I don't need bridesmaids and a reception and all that, but I was picturing going to the courthouse in regular clothes and it just doesn't seem right. Is that okay? You can wear whatever you want, but I guess I want that little bit of ceremony." She looked so guilty for wanting that and I couldn't stand it.

I leaned over and hugged her.

"Care, you can wear a dinosaur suit if you want to. I don't give a flying fuck. And if you want a bouquet? I'll get you the best damn bouquet ever." I already knew what she'd want in her bouquet because I knew all her favorite flowers.

The tension in her face melted into an adorable smile. I would do anything to make her happy. That's what best friends did.

"What are you going to wear?" she asked. I hadn't thought about that either.

"No idea. I might need you to help me pick something. I'll go shopping with you if you want." Her cheeks got red.

"What?" I asked.

"Um, I might have already picked a dress out at a shop. It's way too much money, but I figured I might as well. I mean, if and when I eventually do this again, I'll probably want something else. Styles change so fast, so I don't think what I want now will be what I want when I'm thirty. So I might as well use it now, right?"

"Sounds good," I said. I had never thought about wedding dresses like that, so I couldn't relate, but I was going to pretend and nod and smile through this whole thing. She was doing this huge thing for me and I wanted her to be happy while we were doing it.

"I can go with you to see it, if you want." I'd never thought about going to a wedding dress shop, but now I was curious. I was curious about all of this stuff now.

"Really? I trust you to tell me if it looks awful on me." Nothing had ever looked awful on her, and I would tell her that too, but I agreed for now. The idea of seeing Cara in a wedding dress hit me with a bolt of longing. I wanted to see it. I wanted to see her.

"It'll be fun," I said, even though I wasn't sure if that was the right word. We went back to the food and didn't talk for a while. I was starting to think about what I might want. After a few minutes of pondering, I still had no idea. I'd have to try something on, I guess. Maybe I'd try a dress on at the shop. What the hell, why not? You didn't wear a wedding dress every day. Might as well take my opportunity. Treat it like Halloween.

When we had eaten as much as we could and had nearly finished the bottle of wine, we ended up laying on the grass and staring up at the sky.

"Once you get all of your bills and shit taken care of, what are you going to do with the money?" she asked.

"I hadn't thought that far ahead. I've only gotten to the 'getting out of debt' stage. I'm not sure. I've never really had a lot of money, so I'm just used to not buying things. I don't even know how to indulge, isn't that sad?" My parents had always been on the lower end of middle class, and we'd flirted with the poverty line more than a few times.

"If I had it, I'd buy lots of fancy cheese and maybe a better apartment and there's this Kate Spade bag I've been looking at for like a year, but can't justify buying." I turned my head to look at her.

"Which one?" She got out her phone and showed me. I committed it to memory and hoped that when I went online that I could find the right one because I was getting her that damn bag.

"Other than that, maybe traveling? I want to go so many places." Right, traveling. That would be cool.

"We can take a honeymoon. That's another perk of getting married. We get to go on a trip. Since I don't have a job, I can go anytime." In fact, that was a great idea and I was going to start looking at plane tickets as soon as I got back.

"Could we?" Her voice was so hopeful. Looks like we'd found a few ways to spend my money.

"Absolutely. It'll be a friendship honeymoon. Best friends go on trips all the time. Where do you want to go?" She let out a breath and laughed.

"I have no idea."

"Me neither," I said.

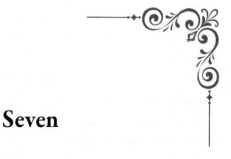

Seven

One proposal down, one to go. We still had to get a marriage license, Cara needed her dress, I needed something to wear, and then we needed to get our asses to the courthouse and make this sucker official.

It was hard keeping everything from my other friends. Ansel might be kind of a pain in the ass sometimes, but he knew how to keep a damn secret. He was like a vault.

I tried to keep the conversations casual, saying that I was busy looking for a job and would get back to them when I could. A lot of them were in school, or working multiple jobs, or dealing with bad mental health episodes, so we didn't get to see each other as often as I would like. I saw Ansel and Cara the most.

I told my mom about the proposal and I thought she was crying on the other end of the line.

"Mom, you know this was just for the money, right? And that you hate weddings and all that go with them?" My parents were deeply in love, but didn't show it the way a lot of people did. I'd grown up used to it, but had learned that other people's parents didn't have pretend fights just for fun and then burst out laughing when neither of them could keep a straight face.

"I know," she said, and I heard a sound like she was blowing her nose. "I'm just so happy for both of you. I know it's not real, but you're my girls and you're taking care of each other. What more could a mother ask for?"

"You're ridiculous," I said, but now I was getting emotional.

"You're going to send us pictures, right?" she said.

"I don't know. If someone takes some. This whole thing is turning into a big production. I hope it doesn't get out of hand. I just want to get it done. Did you talk to the financial guy?" My mom had offered to make the first contact with the financial planner who was in charge of paying out the account. I wondered how many other clients he had with stipulations like mine.

"Yeah, he was out, but I left a message with his assistant. I'll deal with it for you. That's my job." I was relieved, because all that money stuff made me so anxious that my brain literally shut down and I couldn't think when people started talking about things like annuities and IRAs.

"Thank you so much. That's a lot."

"I know. Being an adult is hard sometimes, isn't it?" Now I felt like I was going to cry for a different reason.

"And sometimes you still need your mom," I said, choking up a little.

"Oh, baby. You need to come and see us some more. Get on a bus, we'll pick you up at the station." I hadn't been back to see them in a while, and I definitely had guilt about it.

"I'll bring Cara after we get married. We can have a fake reception at the house." My mom made a little sound of glee.

"I'm so glad you said that. I was dying to ask if we could do something. We could do it in the barn and set up tables and have a cake and –"

"Whoa, Mom." I had to cut her off. "We're not going to need a cake and all that. This is a fake wedding, right? Fake." I was probably going to get tired of telling my parents this wasn't real.

"Oh, I know. But I still think we should have cake. Every special occasion deserves cake." She knew how to make me cave.

"I know you're right. Okay, there can be cake."

"And maybe some pretty lights and decorations?" This was going to be a disaster.

"You're pushing it, Mom. Let me talk to Cara and see what she wants to do. She might not want to do anything but having lasagna with the family." My parents always made lasagna on Friday nights and Cara had spent more of those nights with my family than her own. She could actually make my mother's recipe better than I could. I had never been much of a cook, but she had a gift for it.

"Fine, fine. Talk to your fiancée." I could tell she was smiling.

Technically, Cara was my fiancée, so I wasn't going to argue with her. I also kind of liked hearing Cara referred to as my fiancée. No idea why. It just sounded good.

"I will," I said and then she put me on with Dad, who wanted to build us both bookshelves until I told him that we weren't living together, and neither of our apartments was big enough for bookshelves. He was grumpy about that and downgraded his ideas to making us book ends.

At last I got off the phone with him and called Cara.

"My dad wants to make us bookshelves and my mom wants to throw us a reception, how are you?" I said in a rush.

"Um, not great. My landlord says that his son is coming back to live with him and he wants my apartment for his son to live in, so he's giving me some time to find a new place, but not much."

"Wait, what? He's kicking you out?" She made a sound that was almost a sob.

"I'm on a month-to-month lease. So he can." Wow. That was shitty.

"How long do you have?"

"Thirty days." I swore. That wasn't long at all.

"Fuck, Cara. I'm so sorry. I wish I could say that you could live here, but there's only the two bedrooms and my landlord is an asshole." Plus, I didn't think my roommate was going to go for that at all.

"It's okay, it's not your responsibility. But it means I might need more than the twenty thousand." Oh, right. The money.

"You can have as much as you need. Any amount. You can have all of it."

"Lo, I can't take all your money. I just can't. I think I'll be fine to find a place. I'll just have to lower my standards, that's all. It'll be fine. I'm sorry for dumping on you."

"Care, you're my best friend and my fake fiancée. You're never dumping on me. I'm here for you. For everything." I wished I could put my arms around her right now and hug her until she didn't need me to hug her anymore.

"I know. I still feel like I'm taking advantage or I'm a burden. Thanks, Mom and Dad for fucking me up like that." Whenever she talked about the damage her parents had done, I wanted to get on a bus, go to their house and scream at them all the nasty things I had ever thought about them. And then I remembered that they didn't deserve it. They deserved to be wiped from our lives. Exiled. Forgotten. Cara had parents, and their names were Tim and Grace Bowman.

"You're never a burden," I said.

"Thanks, Lo. Do you mind if I come over? I know it's crowded there, but I don't want to be at my place right now. And maybe you can help me look for apartments?"

"Yes, come over. Right now." I didn't care if Lisa didn't like it. My best friend fiancée needed me. Friendiancee? The words didn't matter. Cara needed me.

"I BROUGHT STUFF," SHE said, when I answered the door. "Since I was crashing, I thought I would bring dinner. Is sushi okay?" I had been craving it actually, so that was great. Like she'd read my mind.

"You're the best," I said, taking the bag of sushi and giving her a hug.

"No, but I try." She kept her voice down as we walked up the stairs and dashed through the living room to get to the back of the house where my room was. Lisa had taken the nicer, bigger room at the front of the apartment, but I was closer to the bathroom, so I didn't have to stumble through the entire house when I had to pee at 3 am. So who was the winner?

"Is she here?" she whispered as I closed the door to my room.

"I think so? It's hard to tell. She's really quiet and spends most of her time listening to music with those giant noise-cancelling headphones, or sometimes she disappears for like three days. I never really know, so I never feel comfortable running around the house in my underwear. It's kind of annoying." She nodded and flopped down on my bed.

"Sometimes I think about getting a roommate because it would be cheaper, but then I remember that I'd be living with a stranger and that would be awful." I lay down beside her. My bed wasn't as big as hers, so we were smushed a little.

"Yeah, you're right. I should have vetted potential roommate candidates, but I was desperate and right out of college and she seemed nice. I mean, she's not horrible. It could be so much worse. Most of the time I don't even know she's there, which I guess is good." Cara turned on her side and popped open the box of spicy salmon and avocado rolls. I broke our chopsticks apart and she handed me my sweet potato and avocado roll and box of spring rolls to share.

"I don't want to move. I like my neighborhood. I don't like my apartment, but I wish I could afford to stay there. Now I'm going to have to find a different route to work and new takeout places." She pouted and stabbed a piece of sushi with her chopsticks before dipping it in soy sauce and popping it into her mouth.

"That sucks. I wish you could move in here, but Lisa is distantly related to the guy who owns this place, so I'm pretty sure she's not going anywhere and that's why the rent is so low." I had it so much better than a lot of my friends. Ansel was cursed by terrible apartments. Every single one he'd lived in had been more awful than the last. And he wasn't renting cheap shitholes either. One of his places had been infested with bedbugs even though it was brand-new, one had had a roof cave in, and one had been condemned right after he moved in. He had other traumas as well, so we had all wondered if he just had bad taste in apartments, or if he was born under the wrong star.

"That's okay. I'll figure it out. Now that I don't have to worry about school, I can put all my extra money to rent. What little extra I have." She groaned and pulled her laptop out of her bag after setting her sushi aside. I was still busy stuffing my face with mine.

"So let's see where my next crappy apartment is going to be." I sat up and we put the laptop between us and started looking.

Immediately, things looked grim. Real grim.

"This is a closet. Like, an actual closet that has somehow been turned into an apartment. And I don't think I could even fit in that shower. Also, where is the stove?" We clicked and clicked, and it was bad. I'd hoped we would find even one that might be acceptable, but no such luck.

"We don't have to find one right now. You've got a little time. We can try again tomorrow," I said, closing the laptop so Cara would stop clicking and getting sadder and sadder. Her shoulders had sagged and I could tell she was on the verge of tears.

"We'll figure this out. Worst case? I'll give you some more money to get a better place." She started to protest, but I put my hand up.

"I'm not letting you live in a cockroach-infested closet when I can prevent that from happening. You're my friendiancee. So deal with it." She snorted.

"Friendiancee? Is that what I am?"

"Yup. And I'm yours." Even though I didn't have my ring on. "Speaking of that, when is this grand proposal happening? Because I want something shiny on my finger." She looked down at her hand where she'd been spinning her ring around and around.

"You just have to be patient. I'm working on it. I got a little sidetracked with this apartment thing." Ouch, now I felt like a bitch.

"I'm sorry, I shouldn't have put that much pressure on you about it. I know we've both got other shit going on." A lot of other shit.

"I know," she said, leaning back on my pillows and closing her eyes. "I just want things to stand still for a while. Just stand still and breathe and not have to worry so much. Just for a while." I wanted that too, so I copied her position and closed my eyes.

"We're still right now, together." She let out a deep breath and I snuck a peek at her.

"You're right, we are. This is nice. I always feel so much calmer when I'm with you. You make everything slow down a little." She did the same for me. Whenever I was flipping out about something, I knew that if I talked to Cara, she would sit me down and tell me that it was going to be okay and help me come up with a game plan with bullet points to tackle whatever the problem was that I was flipping out about in the first place. I didn't know what I would do without her.

High school had been so hard without her. We'd tried to keep in touch, but things happened and we just weren't in each other's lives anymore. But even if we hadn't talked for months, when we did talk, it was as if we'd started in the middle of a sentence that had never ended. A sentence that, if I had my way, would go on forever. I didn't know where my life was going to take me, but I knew that I wanted Cara by my side for the whole ride.

"Do you want to stay over?" I asked, hoping she would say yes. She'd said she didn't have to work until tomorrow afternoon, so I hoped that was an incentive.

"Can I?" What a silly question.

"If you let me finish the spring rolls."

She smiled and my heart did a little twirl.

"Deal."

Eight

That night was the same as the other night when we'd shared her bed. Only this time, she threw her leg over mine and put her arm across my chest. As if she was cuddling with me in her sleep. I hadn't said anything about the last time because I didn't want her to feel weird about it. She couldn't control what her body did when she wasn't awake. Her warm skin pressed against mine, since we were only wearing tank tops and shorts, so there was a ton of skin exposure.

I was tired and I wanted to sleep, but I didn't think I could. I maneuvered onto my side, with Cara's limbs still wrapped around me. Would it be bad if I put my arms on her too? Or if I snuggled into her? Since I was awake, was that okay? I didn't know, but I wanted to be close to her. I liked sleeping next to Cara, even if she hogged the bed and wouldn't let go of me. There was a comfort in knowing another person was going to be there when you woke up.

I wasn't alone.

I hoped Cara wouldn't mind as I wiggled closer to her and rested my forehead against hers. As if she approved, she made a little happy sighing noise in her sleep.

"Goodnight friendiancee," I whispered and finally let myself fall asleep.

By the time I woke up the next morning, I was alone in my bed again, but I could hear singing in the kitchen and the sound of sizzling bacon.

I hoped Lisa wasn't around, or else she was going to have a fit. She did not like it when I even went near the kitchen. I had no idea why, but every time I used the kitchen, I got passive aggressive notes on my door asking if I could not touch her stuff (I didn't touch her stuff), or not load the dishwasher THAT way (I didn't know what way she was doing it), or not take her spices (I had never taken her spices), so a lot of times I made something in the microwave as quickly as I could and scurried back to my room.

The singing got louder as I stretched in bed. I must have slept well because I couldn't remember waking up a bunch of times like I usually did. I also had to pee like hell.

I stumbled out of bed and to the bathroom before heading to the kitchen to see what was happening. Cara had her hair piled up on her head in the perfect messy twist and was swiveling her hips to a song that was playing in her head as she whipped some eggs together in a bowl.

"What's going on in here?" I asked, and she realized I was there and almost dropped the bowl.

"Oh, you're awake." I leaned against the counter and crossed my arms. Her face got a little red as she stopped whipping the eggs.

"Good morning," I said, motioning for her to hand me the bowl. "Your bacon is going to burn." She blinked once and then cursed, rushing to turn the bacon over so it didn't turn black.

"Sorry, you were so out of it that I didn't think you were going to be up for a while. I was going to bring you breakfast in bed like a good friendiancee should." I clumsily whipped the eggs as best

I could until they were combined and passed them back to Cara, who poured them in a pan to be scrambled.

"That's really cute, Cara, but you don't have to do stuff like that." She didn't owe me anything.

"I know, but I wanted to. It sounded like fun." She moved the eggs around in the pan as the toaster went off. "Can you get that out?" I nodded and grabbed the plates that she'd set out, and stacked the toast on them. She'd found a tray to carry everything into the bedroom that I was ninety-nine percent sure wasn't mine and belonged to Lisa. I almost said something, but I didn't want to kill her joy. I would take the heat from Lisa if she somehow found out we'd used her tray and got pissy about it.

Cara dished the breakfast up on the plates, and I filled wine glasses with orange juice to be extra fancy. By the time we were done, the tray was so heavy that we both had to carry it so one of us didn't drop it.

"Shit, I forgot butter," she said, about to get up, but I stopped her.

"I got it." The second I returned with the butter, Cara asked me if I could get the jam, and then the salt and pepper. I laughed and brought her everything she wanted.

"I'm such a pain in the ass," she said.

"But you're my pain in the ass. I mean, at least legally." She pointed her fork at me.

"Not yet." I narrowed my eyes.

"You backing out on me, Care?" She smirked.

"Maybe I'm looking at other options."

"What kind of options?"

"Maybe you're not the only one who wants a trophy wife," she said. "I could leverage this offer into others." I burst out laughing.

"Okay, so who are the lucky dudes? Or not-dudes?" Cara and I hadn't really talked about what people would think about the two of us being married. Of course, she was straight and it would look like she wasn't when she married me, but that didn't appear to bother her at all.

"Oh, a *very* dashing gentleman offered for my hand, and I'm considering. He's a lawyer-billionaire-cowboy and his name is Thaddeus McRich Goldblood XIV." I was dying. I was laughing so hard that I had to hold onto my dresser to stay upright.

"I have so many questions," I said, barely getting the words out.

"He also owns several lions, castles, helicopters, and at least one spaceship." She was playing this up with a complete straight face and it was so much funnier that way. This wasn't the first time Cara made me laugh so hard that I thought I was going to rupture a lung or two.

"Only one spaceship?" I said, wiping my eyes.

"He's building a second as we speak. We'll go to Mars for our honeymoon. That is, if I accept his offer." I sat down on the bed and gulped down some orange juice.

"Well, that's a lot to compete with. I'm not a billionaire or a cowboy and I don't have a spaceship or a tiger." Cara huffed dramatically.

"Then what *do* you have?"

"Money?" I said. "And I do love you. Not in a marriage way, but that still counts, I think. And I'm really good at shoulder rubs." She nodded seriously.

"That is a lot to consider. Give me a moment." She pretended to be deep in thought, but her hand was fiddling with something under the pillow.

"Okay," she said, nodding decisively. "I have made my decision."

"And?" I said. I had a feeling I knew what she was doing, and my heart had started pounding a heavy rhythm. Was she?

"And I have chosen you, Loren Alyssa Bowman. Will you marry me?" She brought out the ring and held it out to me. My hands shook, and I thought I was going to cry and laugh at the same time.

I couldn't even speak. My heart was going berserk in my chest and I didn't know how to calm it down. I didn't know how to calm *me* down.

"Yes," I finally said, my voice choked with emotion. My eyes burned and my chest was so tight, it was as if my organs had expanded and were too big to fit anymore.

Cara put the ring on my trembling finger. I held my hand up and tilted it back and forth. The ring was just so pretty and I was happy to finally have it on my hand.

My focus went from the ring to Cara's smile and I was hit with a thousand emotions, all of them intense, some of them confusing. A thousand voices were screaming in my brain, all shouting different things, a cacophony of joy and elation.

"I know it wasn't fancy, but we're not fancy, so there you go," Cara said, and I wanted to scream and jump up and down and drink a shot and dive into a lake and do a bazillion other things. There was too much inside and I had to let some of it out.

"Are you okay?" she asked, and I realized I was crying, so I wiped the tears.

"Yeah, I'm fine," I said and started to get a little embarrassed about my outlandish reaction, even if she had no idea what was going on inside me. I took a few deep breaths and then tried to distract myself with food.

"You did a good job," I said, and she smiled.

"Good. You were kinda quiet there, so I was worried I'd been too much of a dork." She wasn't a dork. She was my best friend and I loved her more than anything.

"No, it was perfect," I said. It was just the kind of proposal I'd want if I was really getting married, but this was probably the only one I'd ever get, so I was going to treasure it.

The sparkle of the ring kept distracting me as we ate, and I couldn't stop looking at it.

"It took me a while to get used to," Cara said, catching me looking at my newly bedazzled finger.

I held my hand out and she put her left hand next to mine. I snuck a picture with my phone.

"You're not going to post that, are you?" she asked.

"No. I just wanted to have it. That's something else we need to discuss. I know we're going to tell close friends and so forth, but are we going to announce this on social media or anything?" Cara munched on some bacon and thought about it.

"I don't see where it would come up? Like, we don't have to post anything publicly and then no one will even know. If we posted even something vague, I think we'd have to deal with way too many questions. Don't you think?" I wasn't sure what I thought, but I did know I didn't want her to do anything she wasn't comfortable with.

"Yeah, probably. And you're not, you know, queer, so that would lead to a lot of questions for you to answer." In an ideal world, we wouldn't have to worry about that, but it wasn't, and I wondered what she thought about it all.

"I don't mind," she said in a low voice. "People are going to think whatever they want, but it doesn't matter to me. I don't care."

She wouldn't look at me, and her face was a little red, but her voice was determined. Cara raised her chin and met my eyes.

"It doesn't matter," she said again, and I wasn't sure if she was trying to convince me or herself. I wasn't going to argue or press her about it. That was something she had to decide.

"Okay," I said, but I guess I didn't sound sure enough. She grabbed my left hand with her left and squeezed until the ring cut into my finger. A little drop of pain.

"I love you, Loren. Every part of you." The tears were threatening to make their appearance again. I remembered when I came out to her. She'd sat there for a few seconds, gave me a hug, told me she loved me, and asked which female celebrities I thought were hot. And that was it. Ever since then she'd been on board with my life. No conditions. No "I love you even if you're queer." Just "I love you and you are queer and I love your queerness because it's a part of you."

"Thanks," I said, my voice choked.

"Anytime you need a reminder, you let me know." She put her arms out for a hug and I fell into her, so we ended up horizontal on the bed, laughing. I spit out some of her hair from my mouth and wiped my eyes.

"You're the best. The best friendiancee a girl could ask for," I said.

"Ditto."

Nine

My mom called me back a day later when she'd finally gotten in touch with the financial planner who was in charge of disbursing the inheritance. All I needed was a certified copy of the marriage certificate and then there would either be a check with my name on it sent, or a wire transfer to my bank account. I also needed to fill out some paperwork that he was sending me and get my signature notarized. It was all so official and adult and it started hitting me what this money was going to mean.

It was no small amount. For someone who had never grown up with a whole lot, it was probably a lot more than for someone else who had. I knew that I shouldn't blow it. I wasn't going to be like those people who won the lottery and burned through the money in a year and ended up bankrupt. I wouldn't let that be me.

This money was going to change my life, change Cara's life too. I knew she wasn't going to want me to give her more than her tuition, but I was definitely plotting how I could give her some extra so that she wouldn't have to stress so much about paying for everything else. I also wasn't going to let her pay me back, but she didn't know that yet.

Oh, and I was going to buy her that bag. That was probably the first thing I was going to do. For myself, I considered getting a better apartment, but I wanted to take care of the immediate needs like my car and groceries and this month's rent. I could always find a new apartment later. I needed to stop the immediate hemorrhaging and then deal with the rest of the wounds.

I just wanted to be stable for a while. Just go a few months paying my bills on time and not stressing too much if I decided to order sushi. Big dreams, I had.

Cara had set an appointment to go look at the dress she wanted and I was wondering when we were actually going to do the damn thing because days were going by and I just wanted to have this done with. Still, I didn't want to push her, because I didn't want her to run for the hills. Or to ruin our friendship. That absolutely could not happen. The money meant nothing compared to losing her. I couldn't begin to imagine my life without her. I'd give her every single cent to stop that from happening.

The day before Cara's appointment, I was online scrolling through potential jobs when Lisa knocked on my door. She only did that if there was an emergency, or she needed the rent check, which wasn't due for a couple of weeks, so I had no idea what it was. My heart started to pound.

I got up and opened the door, but I couldn't tell what was up from her expression. Lisa was one of those people who always looked a little grim. I didn't think I'd ever seen her smile.

"Hey, what's up?" I asked, pretending to be calm and casual. Totally cool. Not freaking out at all.

"So, I'm moving out in three weeks. You can either keep the place and pay the full rent, or find someone else. Up to you." I blinked at her for a few seconds.

"You're moving out?" She'd said it so fast that my brain needed a second to catch up.

"I'm subletting in a better neighborhood. I'm going to be packing up most of my stuff, so make sure you return anything you might have borrowed." I hadn't borrowed any of her shit and she knew that.

"Oh, okay," I said. Great, just great. She gave me a tight little smirky smile and went back down the hall to her room and slammed the door.

So much for standing still. Now I had to figure out if I was going to stay or go. The rent was pretty reasonable, so I could stay now that I was getting the inheritance money, so I didn't have to panic too much. Plus, I could move into the nicer bedroom once Lisa vacated it. Maybe I could turn the spare into an office or something. Or get a dog. That would be nice.

Plus, having the place to myself? Not so bad. I was already thinking about redecorating. This could be great. I could make this work.

And then I remembered Cara. Holy shit, another incredible idea. I called her right away.

"Have you found an apartment yet?" I asked by way of a greeting. I was vibrating with excitement again.

"Uh, no. Not really. I did find a nice box in the basement, though, so I might live there." I didn't have time to laugh at her joke.

"You can move in with me. Lisa's moving out and I can deal with the rent on my own, but you need a place and I have one," I said all in a rush. I wished she was with me in person so I could hug her and we could jump up and down and celebrate.

"Wait, really?" she said after a few seconds of silence.

"Yes! Then I won't have to worry about getting along with a roommate because we get along already. It's totally perfect." Yet another good idea. I was having all kinds of them lately. And saving not just my own ass, but my best friend's.

"Are you sure about that?" Was she serious?

"Cara. You're my best friend. Living with you would literally be the best thing. I mean, I don't want to pressure you. But if you want to live here, you can move in with me." I probably should have opened with that instead of throwing the idea at her as if I'd already decided she should do it. That was always one of my issues. I got a little too enthusiastic and started running before I'd even made a plan.

"Oh, wow, yeah. I mean, I'd love to live with you, Lo. I can't think of anything better. If you're sure."

"I couldn't be more sure if I tried."

"Holy crap, that is amazing. I don't have to live in a box." I laughed.

"Nope. You can have your very own room with walls and everything."

"How will I handle living in such luxury?"

"Um, don't hate me, but I'm going to move into the other room, if that's okay?" I probably should have let her pick, but I was a little selfish.

"No, that's fine. It's your place. I'm used to having a small room. You know this." I did. We talked some more about the rent and when she was going to move in and adding her to the lease and so forth.

"We can get a cat. Or a bunny. Or a dog," I said and Cara laughed.

"Let's just see if we can live together without ending our friendship first. Spending the night is one thing, seeing someone every single day is another." I rolled my eyes.

"Care. You practically lived at my house when we were kids. I think we can handle this. Plus, it's not like we're sharing a room. Just the kitchen and bathroom and so forth. It's going to be fine. We've got this." She sighed.

"You're right. You're totally right. I'm just being weird. Okay, so we're getting married and living together now?" I guess we were.

"Yup. You're gonna be my live-in wife." It was the first time I'd referred to her as my wife and the word had never struck me as anything special until now. But pairing that word with Cara was something else. It hit me just as hard as when she'd proposed and put the ring on my finger.

This was fake. We weren't getting real married. I had to keep reminding myself of that and stop getting all carried away and swept up. I couldn't let things get out of hand. I had to slow my roll.

"Huh, I guess I am," she said. "That's so weird. I haven't thought of myself as someone's wife. I mean, even if we're just doing it for money and getting it annulled. Oh, you're coming to my appointment, right?"

"Yeah, absolutely." I still wasn't sure how I felt about the whole dress thing, but anything to get her excited.

"Great. Listen, I've got to go right now, but I'll see you on Tuesday? You know where the place is, right?" I didn't but I had GPS in my phone.

"See you then, Care," I said and hung up. The front door slammed and I realized that Lisa had left, so I could head to the kitchen to make something to eat. I couldn't believe in a few weeks that she was going to be gone, Cara was taking her place, and all of my money problems were going to be solved.

Life was pretty fucking great right now.

Ten

"Are you sure about this?" I asked as I looked at the window display in front of the dress shop. It wasn't what I expected. Instead of a cupcake fluff-fest, it was a little more edgy. The mannequin in the window had a high-low dress with a hint of pink in the skirt that was posed next to a moped and had a set of motorcycle boots on the other side. Okay, this was not your average dress shop.

"Yeah, I am," Cara said, reaching out and holding the door for me. "Come on, this is going to be fun."

I took a deep breath and walked into the shop. It was light and bright, but didn't feel stuffy. There were comfy couches and chairs everywhere and at one end of the shop were mirrors and even a little runway. Several other people were already browsing as soft music played from hidden speakers. I stopped to listen and realized it was Etta James. Nice.

"Welcome to Love and Lace, do you have an appointment?" We both turned to find a consultant standing near us. She wore a black lace t-shirt with a leather skirt and black booties. It was a nice contrast to all the white around.

"Yes, I have an appointment. Cara Simms?" The consultant held up a tablet and scrolled.

"Great, you're all checked in. I'm Chloe and I'll be working with you today. Who have you brought with you?" Cara looked at me and I looked at her and then she looked back at Chloe.

"This is my fiancée, Loren," Cara said, and I almost fell over. I mean, technically I was, but I didn't think she was going to be so open about it.

"Congratulations to you both," Chloe said, beaming at both of us. "Now do you want to get a dress as well, or are you looking for something else?" I still couldn't get over the fact that Cara had called me her fiancée in public for the first time.

"Oh, uh, I don't know," I mumbled.

"That's absolutely fine. You can look around and see what you might like and we'll make another appointment. Now, when is the big day?" Cara and I shared a look.

"As soon as possible," I said, and Chloe laughed.

"Okay, that makes things a little different. Usually gowns have to be ordered months in advance, but I can show you what we've got in stock. Now, do you want to see her in the dress, Loren?" Cara turned to me.

"I don't think I can pick without you," she said, and my heart did a little wiggle of joy. I loved that she needed my opinion to make this decision. Plus, Cara looked amazing in everything, so it was going to be a good time. I'd been totally anxious and apprehensive, but now I was getting excited. Little birds were flapping their wings in my stomach. Not butterflies, these flutters were bigger than that.

"You two are so sweet, this is going to be fun." Chloe clapped her hands happily and I was glad she was almost as into this as I was. Part of me had been a little worried we might run into a homophobic consultant. You never knew when anti-queerness was going to rear its nasty head, but Chloe seemed totally on board and, after glancing around again, I noticed something you might not see in a more conservative bridal shop: white suits. There was a whole wall of them, some that had matching skirts that were cut so as to be open in the front to show the pants, and then that draped into the back. A mannequin had one of the contraptions on that had a sweeping train bedazzled with rhinestones and lace. Now THAT was a look.

Chloe took us through the whole shop, asking Cara about her style, what she wanted to look like on the day, whether or not she wanted pure white or was open to colors (of which there were many), and if she wanted to wear a veil or not.

"I don't think I want a veil. It's going to be more casual," she said. Her hands were trembling and there was panic in her eyes. She was getting overwhelmed, I could tell, so I reached out and squeezed her fingers.

"It's okay, Care, you don't have to decide now. I can take pictures of you in each dress and then you can sit down and do pro and con lists for each one." Her face relaxed and she leaned into me.

"Thank you. I don't know how I could do this without you."

"Okay, you have to stop. I can't," Chloe said, shaking her head at us. "You're just too cute." For some reason, I didn't care that she thought we were a romantic couple. Close friendship could often look like that, especially when girls were concerned. And it wasn't like I didn't love Cara. I did. I loved her more than I'd ever loved anyone, no question. I didn't dare spoil Chloe's heart-eyes by telling her we were just faking this for money. If she was buying it and it made her happy, who cared? Lots of people were going to think we were a couple, so what did it matter if this random bridal consultant thought so?

Cara pointed to a few dresses that caught her eye and then went with Chloe into the changing room. I took my seat on a plush off-white couch and waited. There was another group seated near me that looked to be a girl who had brought literally everyone she had ever met to help her make this decision. Mom, grandmother, aunts, cousins, best friends, etc. The works. I shuddered as she came out in a dress that she clearly loved, judging from the smile beaming on her face, but was promptly shut down by nearly everyone. Her shoulders crumpled and she shuffled sadly back to the dressing room. A little voice inside me wanted to pipe up and tell her that those people didn't know what they were talking about and that she had looked amazing, but it wasn't my place to interfere. Still, I tried to shoot her a sympathetic look when she came out in the next dress which was boring as fuck, but her whole group clapped as if it was the most beautiful dress ever created. Blah city. I couldn't watch anymore, and Chloe poked her head out of the dressing room to tell me that Cara was coming out in the first dress.

My hands started to shake and I couldn't breathe. I clutched my fingers together and tried to calm myself. Why was I getting so worked up? Maybe they pumped something through the air here, along with the subtle scents of lemons and lavender.

"Here she comes," Chloe said, holding the door open and stepping aside to let Cara walk out.

"Oh, shit," I said in a whisper.

"Is it too much?" Cara said, biting her bottom lip.

I shook my head, unable to form words.

"Is that good?" she asked, looking down at the flowing skirt that was draped perfectly and fell to the floor. The top had gauzy straps that rested on her shoulders and light pink lace flowers on the bodice. It was stunning and subtle at the same time and fit her body like a glove. As if it was made for her. Chloe had pulled her hair back in a loose bun that was just haphazard enough to be perfect.

"I wasn't sure about the pink, but..." Cara said, brushing her hand across the top of the bodice, right where the dress ended and the skin of her upper chest was revealed. She was looking for something from me, but I just couldn't seem to make words come from my mouth.

"I'm going to take a wild guess and say that she likes it," Chloe said. "Let me know if I'm wrong, but I'm pretty sure that's what that look on her face means." I nodded slowly.

"It's perfect," I finally said. My mouth was dry and I had to swallow a few times.

"Is it?" she asked, twirling around and showing me the incredible movement of the skirt.

"Yeah," I said, not even realizing I'd gotten up and had walked up the steps to the little platform she was on in front of the mirrors.

"You look so pretty," I said, and I found tears coming from my eyes.

"Do I?" she asked, a question still in her voice.

"You do. I promise."

"Do you apple pie promise?" she said and a laugh bubbled out of my throat. When we were kids, we'd decided to have something bigger than a pinkie promise and apple pie was both of our favorite things at the time, so we swore on apple pie instead. Since then our tastes had changed and I was more of an ice cream girl, but the sentiment was the same.

I reached out and took both of her hands.

"I apple pie promise." She squeezed my hands back and looked over her shoulder at the mirror.

"I can't pick this one, Lo. It's the first one I've tried on. You can't pick the first one." Chloe cleared her throat.

"Many brides find that their first instinct is the right one and end up coming back to the first dress even after trying on dozens of others. Just something to keep in mind." Cara turned her head to the side and swished the dress a little. I let go of one of her hands and motioned for her to twirl under my arm. She did, giggling a little.

"It twirls perfectly, which is very important," I said, keeping my face serious.

"Well, that's good to know. But I still want to try on more dresses." I didn't care if she wanted to try on every damn thing in the whole entire store. Twice. I would stay here with her. I would come back the next day and the next forever if she wanted. I'd move in to this store.

"How are we doing over here?" said a husky voice. I turned to find a woman in black leather pants, a gauzy black tank, and a blazer. Her hair was bleached white and undercut on one side. I got immediate queer vibes, especially when I saw that she had an industrial ear piercing on the undercut side. The queer points were racking up.

"Good," Chloe said. "Cara, Lo, this is Maeve, the owner of the store."

"Oh, wow, it's nice to meet you," Cara said, shaking Maeve's hand. I also shook her hand.

"I have to say, that dress isn't for everyone, but you're rocking it. I love that touch of pink," Maeve said, looking Cara up and down. I swear, Cara was blushing.

"Me too," I said, moving to stand closer to Cara. I had the urge to put my arm around her, or hold up the hand with her ring on it.

"It's like it was made for you," Maeve said, ignoring me. "Is this the first one you've tried on?" Cara nodded.

"Well, we might have hit a home run, what do you think?" Cara said that she loved the dress, but didn't think she should pick the first dress without trying on any others.

"Sensible. I like that. Well, let me know if there's anything you need. Can I get you some coffee or tea or perhaps some champagne?" Cara and I exchanged a look.

"Champagne, if you have it." Why not? Made the day more festive.

"You've got it," Maeve said and headed over to a corner where she had a little drink station set up with a coffeemaker, kettle, and an iced bucket with several mini bottles of champagne. Wow, classy.

She popped one of the bottles, filled two glasses, and brought them back over.

Cara was comical as she tried to sip the champagne and keep the glass away from the dress.

"I'm guessing if you spill on it, you buy it," she said.

"We're not that mean here," Maeve said, laughing. "I know how to get pretty much any kind of stain out of a wedding dress. Occupational hazard." She smiled and there was a dimple in one of her cheeks. I felt my own cheeks flush a little. She was hot, that was for sure, and she had the effortless confidence of someone who knew exactly who she was and who she wanted to be. I definitely didn't have that, but I wished I could ask Maeve what her secret was and then copy everything she did. Maybe it was the leather?

"Okay, well, let's go ahead and get you in another dress," Chloe said, and Cara handed me her champagne glass.

"Let me know if you need anything else, we're here to help you with whatever you need," Maeve said, touching my shoulder and then moving on to the large group beside me. They were still hemming and hawing, this time about how the bride was going to do her hair and if she was going to wear a garter. I seriously wanted to swoop in and rescue the poor girl. She looked young and lost.

Maeve seemed to assess the situation and swept immediately up to the trembling bride and put her arm around her shoulder and said something in her ear. The bride nodded and Maeve announced that she was taking the bride for a veil consultation in the back and that everyone was going to have to wait. I watched as she tucked the girl under her arm and pulled her away from her family. Brilliant. The poor girl's voice was drowned out over all those opinions and she needed someone in her corner. I hoped Maeve would be able to help her speak up for herself. It was her damn wedding, after all.

I turned my attention back to Cara as she came out in the next dress. It was all over lace with a nude underlay and was pretty, but it didn't grab me the way the first dress did.

"Out of ten," Cara asked as she turned back and forth in the mirror.

"Seven?" I said. "It doesn't have the wow factor of the first one." Cara nodded decisively.

"You're right. Okay, next dress."

Cara must have tried on at least six more dresses before realizing that nothing could top the first one.

"There's just one thing I want before I say yes to that dress," she said with a sly grin on her face.

"And what's that?" I asked.

"For you to try one on." I blinked at her.

"Me?"

"Yup, you." She pointed at me and then crooked her finger. "Come on, humor me." Cara hopped down the stairs and flopped onto the couch, still wearing the last dress she'd tried on. It was a floaty bohemian thing that wouldn't be out of place at a painfully hipster wedding where the groom had a beard and the colors were navy, pink, and wood grain.

"Uhhh," I said, looking at Chloe, who was smiling.

"Come on," she said, gesturing at the racks. "Choose one."

I should have spent the time I'd been waiting for Cara to come out in each dress looking for my own, instead of watching all of the little dramas around me. I'd been more interested in the people than the dresses.

"Okay," I said, but knew it was going to take me a long time to actually pick something.

"Come with me," Chloe said, heading down the stairs to the opposite corner of the shop. "I have something I think you might like."

I trailed after her and watched as she pulled two items off a rack.

"What do you think about separates?"

I looked at the two pieces she'd pulled. One was a tulle skirt that was high in the front and long in the back and fluffed out just a little bit. The top was a white tank with lace over it that formed long sleeves.

"Oh," I said. For a second, I was going to say "no way, put it back," but the longer I looked at it, the more I thought it would work.

"You like?" Chloe said, raising her eyebrows in expectation.

"I do," I said. "I'll try it on." Chloe grinned and marched me back to the dressing room that Cara had used.

"Hurry upppp," Cara said. "The suspense is killing me." She crossed her arms and looked so grumpy that I couldn't help but laugh.

"I've been waiting for you for hours, get a grip." She wrinkled her nose at me and Chloe shoved me in the dressing room. It was large and had a curtain separating two spaces. The larger space behind the curtain had a bench and hooks on the walls. Cara's street clothes were folded and set on the bench. There wasn't a mirror in here. I gave Chloe a look.

"We like to have the big reveal outside of the room. You can't tell much in the small space. It's too cramped and the lighting isn't the best." I wasn't sure I liked that. I didn't want to go out in something that didn't look good.

"We also have some sample undergarments you can put over what you already have if you want." I was wearing a black bra and undies, so I asked for a slip for the tulle skirt, but the white part of the top was going to cover my bra. It dipped in the back and had buttons all the way down, but not low enough to reveal the band of my bra. Someone had been conscious of being able to wear a bra with straps had designed this. I appreciated that.

"Oh, how much is this?" I asked as I stripped off my t-shirt. I wasn't modest, so Chloe helped me carefully get the lace sleeves over my arm and buttoned the back for me.

"Well, it just so happens this is a discontinued design, so both pieces are half off." I turned and looked at her over my shoulder.

"Half off of what?" She finished the buttons and glanced at the tag hanging from one sleeve and then the tag on the skirt.

"So it would be around four hundred for both pieces." I almost choked. I had no idea how much wedding outfits cost. If two simple pieces were this much ON SALE, how much was Cara's dress going to be? I had a moment of panic and had to remind myself that it didn't matter how much they were. I had thousands coming to me soon. Right. I didn't have to buy generic toothpaste anymore. I could get the expensive kind that helped with tooth pain. Speaking of that, I should go and visit a dentist. It had been a while.

I slammed the brakes on that little momentary anxiety attack and slipped out of my jeans and shoes. Chloe helped me step into the slip and then pull the skirt up and get it so it fit right.

"I'm a genius," Chloe whispered. "I should win awards. Just wait 'til you see it." Not that I didn't trust her, but there was one person's opinion on this outfit that I needed, and she was sitting out there waiting for me.

I was getting nervous again. Like this mattered. I was just trying this on, like a costume. That's all this was. A costume. A frilly, lacy costume.

"Come onnnnn," I heard Cara whining.

"She's coming out," Chloe said, sticking her head out and then holding the door for me.

I locked eyes with Cara and she froze, a smile on her face. She sat up slowly, her hand going to her mouth.

I desperately wanted to look in the mirror, but I couldn't stop looking at her.

"Once again, I'm going to take a shot in the dark and say that she likes it. Correct me if I'm wrong," Chloe said, but I ignored her. All I could see was Cara.

"Do you like it?" It was my turn to be uncertain.

Cara got up from the couch, walked up the steps and put her hands on my shoulders.

"Turn around and look at yourself," she said in a quiet voice.

"I can't," I said, laughing a little under my breath.

"It's okay," she said, stepping close to me. "You can look." She pushed at one of my shoulders, so I took a step back and then continued until I did a 180 degree turn. Cara rested her chin on my shoulder.

"You're gorgeous, Lo. So fucking gorgeous."

She was right. The two pieces were... perfect. Utterly perfect. I couldn't have imagined anything better, or more me. It wasn't something I would have picked, but it was completely me.

"Would you like to see them together?" Chloe said. I took my eyes off myself and Cara and remembered that she was there and were in a bridal shop with a bunch of other people. We weren't the only two people in the entire world.

"Come on, Cara, let's get your dress on and you can see how they look together." I didn't want her to leave me, but she squeezed my shoulders and followed Chloe back into the changing room to put her dress on. After what felt like an eternity, she came out and I lost my breath again.

"You're like two cake toppers. I can't even deal," Chloe said, stepping back and examining us as Cara stepped beside me and took my hand.

"Look at us," she said. "Look at us together."

"I know," I said.

Eleven

We stood there forever, just smiling at each other in the mirror until Chloe cleared her throat.

"I'm so sorry to ruin this perfect moment, but my next appointment is coming up. If you'd like, I can ring you up and you can take them today, or you can come back another day. We have a fee for putting things on hold, but don't worry about that." I finally looked at her.

"What?" I had missed half of what she said.

"Don't worry about the hold fee. I'll waive it for you. Don't tell my boss." The last sentence was said in a conspiratorial whisper.

"Oh, wow, thank you," I said.

"Yes, thanks," Cara said. "But I want mine today. I don't think I can walk away from it. I don't want to take it off." I felt the same way.

"I want mine too," I said, being impulsive. "We'll take both of them." Cara made a high-pitched squeal and threw her arms around my neck.

"Thank you for doing this with me, Lo. I knew it was going to be great." I tucked myself around her and held her.

"Thank you for making me try something on," I said. Her hair smelled like sunlight and limes.

"I can't wait to be married," she said, and I knew how she felt.

Maeve ended up coming to check on us again and getting totally excited asking all about our wedding details. I stuttered, but Cara covered for me and said that we were just going to the courthouse and having a party after with my parents. Maeve seemed to understand and didn't ask any other prying questions. Cara's dress needed a few alterations, so we were going to have to leave it there and come back in a few days, and the cost for both dresses made me want to cry, but I pulled out my credit card. None of this was going to matter soon. Money was going to be something I didn't have to worry about. I was so looking forward to that. I couldn't wait to spend that brain space on something else. Maybe I could take up a new hobby?

Cara and I left the shop with my outfit in a garment bag draped over my arm.

"Holy shit, Care. We just bought wedding dresses." I stared at her and she started laughing.

"I know. I can't believe it. This is really happening. We're getting married." The rings escalated things and now the dresses had made things even more intense. How was I going to deal when we went to get our marriage licenses? I was probably going to cry. My period was coming up, so that made sense.

"We're getting married," I said, and the more I said it, the better I felt about it. I got even more giddy than ever when I looked at my ring and then looked at her.

I threw my arms around her, which was hard with the bulky garment bag. She laughed and hugged me back, but didn't let go right away. She held me, and wasn't letting go.

"Are you okay?" I asked, trying to pull back so I could see her face.

"Yeah," she said, slowly pulling back. There was a wrinkle of confusion on her forehead.

"What is it?" She smoothed everything behind a smile and shook her head, but I knew her better. She was hiding something.

"Nothing. Just excited and worried about my dress being right." The alterations were minor; making the straps just a little shorter and taking two inches off the hem of the dress.

"It's going to be perfect. And if it's not, I'll be pissed and start some shit on your behalf." She laughed a little, but it was brief and then something crossed her face again, like the sun sliding behind a group of clouds. Something was up with her, and I needed to know what it was.

A FEW DAYS LATER, WE went back for the dress. Cara tried it on and I nearly fell over again at how gorgeous she was in it. On the hanger, it was a beautiful dress, but when she was wearing it, that dress went to another stratosphere. She made it perfect.

"Everything good?" Maeve was the one fitting it this time. "I like to make sure our alterations department is doing a good job. Plus, I know how to sew and can fix little things on the fly. But this all looks good." Cara turned back and forth and scrutinized every seam until she nodded.

"It'll work," she said, and skipped back to the dressing room to take it off and Maeve followed her to help. I sat on one of the couches and realized the girl at the next mirror was the same one we'd seen with the giant entourage that had dumped on every dress she liked. I couldn't remember exactly what dress she had been in love with, but another consultant was helping her and there was no one on the couch. She'd come alone. I thought about going over and saying something, but that would probably be creepy, so I just averted my eyes so it didn't look like I was staring.

Cara came out with her voluminous garment bag and Maeve shook our hands one last time and said to send her pictures when we were ready.

"We should celebrate," Cara said as we left the shop. There was no way we were getting this thing on and off public transportation, so we were waiting for a car.

"Yeah?" I said. "Celebrate how?"

"Dinner. And drinks. Champagne." Our car pulled up and we stuffed the dress and ourselves into the backseat.

"You can leave this at my house if you need to and then we can go straight from there," I said, and Cara nodded. I gave the driver my address and we both laughed as we tried to make room for ourselves with the bag between us.

"So we need to figure out this whole moving thing," Cara said. Right. Moving. Moving and a wedding and finding a job and paying my bills. Sometimes I wanted to hold my head and scream, but in a few weeks, it was all going to be good and I wouldn't have to worry anymore. At least that was what I was telling myself.

"Do you want to hire a company? I mean, I know everyone would show up and help, but do we really want to do that?" I asked.

"Yeah, you're right. And I refuse to drive a UHaul in Boston again. Never. Again." I agreed. I'd done the same myself and it had been a complete nightmare.

"So we should probably plan the wedding and do that ASAP so you can have the money to hire movers." I was still shaky on the schedule of how this was all going down. I was kind of counting on Cara to handle that part and I'd deal with everything else. My mom had also been up my ass about it because she was totally serious about having a party for us at the house.

"Well, we have the dresses and I have next weekend off. How about Friday?" Friday. That was eight days away. Suddenly I couldn't breathe and my skin flashed hot and then cold.

"Are you okay?" Cara asked.

"Yeah, I think so. That's just so soon." I fiddled with the zipper on the garment bag.

"I hate to remind you, Loren Bowman, but this was *your* idea. Don't tell me you're getting cold feet now." I wasn't. I didn't think I was.

"It's just the enormity of this is kind of crashing down on me and I'm having a moment. I'll be fine." I tried to give her a smile, but I wasn't sure if it was convincing. Cara reached across the bag, squashing it down, and took my hand.

"It's nothing. Like cosigning a loan. Only we'll be wearing fucking awesome dresses. It's just paperwork." I repeated that to myself. Paperwork. It was just paperwork.

"I'm good. I swear," I said, and she let go of my hand.

"SO, THE WEDDING IS going to be next Friday afternoon," I told my mother when I called her that night after our celebratory dinner. We'd gone to a semi-fancy restaurant, had gotten the cheapest champagne they'd had on the menu, and had shared a tiramisu. I'd almost asked her if she wanted to sleep over again, but I could tell Lisa was in a foul mood and would be cold and nasty if Cara stayed. I didn't want to expose her to Lisa's toxicity if I didn't have to.

"Loren. That's eight days away."

"I know. It's soon, but we need to get it done. Cara has to move and we need money for the movers. So that's when it's happening. We're going to get our marriage license on Tuesday and then do it on Friday. It's just signing a piece of paper, it's not a real marriage, Mom." She sighed heavily on the other end of the line.

"I know, I know. You know I don't have any sentiments about marriage, but still. It's going to be an emotional day. You're doing something for yourself and for Cara that not a lot of people would do. You're taking care of each other, and that's a big part of marriage." Who was this woman, and what had she done with my very practical mother?

"I just want to be there," she said in a quiet voice. Cara and I had decided that we didn't really want or need an audience, because, like she had said, this was a contract. You didn't bring an audience when you signed for a new credit card, or took out a loan.

"You want to come?" I asked in disbelief.

"I know I'm being a sap, but I can't help it. Something happens to you when you have children and it warps your heart until you're crying at commercials." We both laughed.

"Does Dad want to come too?" I couldn't see him wanting to witness our sham ceremony, but I hadn't thought my mother would want to be there either.

"Yes, he does. Not to like, 'give you away' or any of that patriarchal crap, but he wants to see it like I do. We went to every single one of your dance recitals and spelling bees and softball games. This is no different." I suppose I could get it when she put it that way.

"Let me check with Cara and then I'll let you know. I'm sure she'll be fine with it, but I don't want to say yes and make her uncomfortable. I still can't believe she's going along with this and isn't bailing. I feel like I almost bailed when we decided on a day." I stopped pacing and sat down on my bed and leaned back on my pillows.

"Why?" Mom asked.

"I don't know. I guess that made it more concrete and real. I keep waiting for this thing to blow up, or for someone to tell me this was all a joke, or to get arrested or something for faking this thing. I guess it just seems too good to be true?"

Mom was quiet for a moment.

"Sometimes that's true. And sometimes you get the best gifts of all when you least expect them, or think you don't deserve them." I had the distinct feeling she was talking about Dad.

"Just don't let doubt ruin something amazing. You deserve good things in life, Loren. You and Cara." There was a lump in my throat and I had to hang up quickly so I didn't cry on the phone. I wiped away a few stray tears and sighed. I wasn't going to let myself ruin this. I couldn't. I wouldn't.

EVEN THOUGH IT TOOK up a lot of real estate in my room, I hung my dress up so I could see it all the time and remember what it was like when I walked out of the dressing room and saw Cara. It made my hands tingle just remembering it.

Lisa moved out way before her deadline. One day I came home and all her shit was gone. Including a lot of the living room furniture, all the kitchen items (including MY pots), and even the shower curtain. What a bitch, but good riddance.

That night I was up until two in the morning moving all my furniture from my room to the room formerly known as Lisa's. I had to clean a lot first. For someone who was so obsessed with everything being clean and in place in the rest of the house, her room was disgusting. I spent half my time scrubbing and getting rid of dust and other... stains. Part of me wondered if I was going to find a body under the floorboards or something. At last I got everything moved and went the living room, which was a fucking disaster. I decided to deal with that one another day. Plus, since Cara was going to move in, we could get our own stuff. And not a couch that we found on the side of the road, either. We could get real stuff. Adult stuff. Stuff that wasn't pre-owned. I was excited about that too.

I got a few more job rejections and finally, FINALLY, an interview. I put on my best outfit and went to the hair salon, but I could tell immediately that I wasn't going to get the job. Firstly, the kind of clientele was upscale and fancy. Chanel and red-soled shoes and perfume that you didn't get at a drugstore. Coifed and traditional and conservative. I got through it, but I knew they weren't going to be calling me back, and I was okay with that after overhearing a client abusing her stylist for doing exactly what the woman had asked for, but the customer decided that it wasn't what she wanted and blamed the stylist for not listening to her. I didn't want to be part of that, even if I was just sitting at the front desk.

I applied for more jobs, widening my net and going for anything that I thought might be interesting, even if I wasn't qualified. The worst they could do was say no to me. I didn't care if I got rejected via email. Didn't matter.

I also thought about other things. Cara was going to school and while I had my bachelor's degree in communication, it hadn't exactly helped me find a job, and it wasn't really what I wanted to do. The idea of managing the social media of company made me want to cry. I just couldn't do it. I wanted to do something that mattered. I didn't want to be just one part of a whole machine whose only purpose was to make rich people richer. Unfortunately, those were most of the jobs that were available to me. Such fun.

On Tuesday afternoon, we went to the courthouse and got our marriage license. The whole thing was truly anticlimactic. We just had to show ID, swear that we wanted to get married, sign, and that was it. No fireworks, no fanfare.

"That was all very... clerical," Cara said, looking at the paper as we walked out.

"I know, right? I don't know what I thought it would be, but not that. It really was like signing for a credit card."

"Still, it's kind of exciting. Just one more step and then it's happening. Is your mom still being weird about the party?" I rolled my eyes. My mom had gone completely berserk with this whole "reception" thing. She said it was going to be a surprise and that we only had to tell her who we wanted to invite, and she would take care of the rest as a present. I'd made some food suggestions, but she'd shushed me and said she'd handle it. I was a little worried.

"Yes, she is. I haven't seen her this excited about anything in ever. I think she might have missed her calling as a party planner." Cara laughed and shook her head.

"Your mom is something else. But I'm kind of happy we're having a party. That will be fun. Is she doing the invites?"

"Well, I figured that I should probably tell people before they get invited to a reception for a wedding they didn't know was happening, so I took the liberty of telling everyone. Ansel is pissed that he's not the best man." Seriously, he was actually upset.

"Do you, uh, mind if he comes?" Cara slid the paper into a folder she'd brought and carefully slid that into her bag. This was one of the most important pieces of paper either of us had ever had.

"No, not at all. It would be kind of fun, since he's the only one who really knows what we're doing." I was pretty sure our other friends had figured out something was up, but hadn't pushed. Sure, Kell had badgered me for half an hour to give her details about every single thing and I'd had to make up a whole story about how one day Cara and I had realized we were meant for each other that I'm pretty sure she didn't buy, but other than that, everyone had been shocked, then supportive, then excited. A few had even asked if we had a registry, which was something I hadn't even thought of.

"I still don't think we need to do the registry thing. It seems weird. Since we're going to be getting piles of money. I'd feel bad asking for stuff from our friends," I said.

"Yeah, I agree. And it's all so sudden, so they don't really have time to figure anything out. I'd feel uncomfortable if they did anything. They're coming to the party and that's enough. Hey, I'm starving, you want to get something to eat?"

Only four days. Four days until our wedding.

Eleven

Cara and I fielded some more questions about our wedding from friends over the next few days and had to tell them that we wanted it to be private. I didn't even want to tell them what time it was in case they decided to show up.

"You know they're probably going to show up. Ansel will tell them," Cara said as we ate pizza in her apartment. The place was even more filled with boxes. We were getting the money next week and she was going to move in on Friday.

"Yeah, he will. He's not the best at keeping secrets. That asshole." Cara handed me a paper towel to wipe pizza sauce off my chin.

"Yes, but we love him."

"Yes. Yes we do."

"So we should have an unpacking party next week, I think. Invite everyone over. Feed them pizza." She held up a slice.

"Sounds great. Use our friends for cheap labor." Cara smacked me with a paper plate.

"They love us. And we would do the same for them." I chomped on a piece of crust.

"We *have* done the same for them." I couldn't count how many friends I'd help move, sometimes multiple times. That was just what happened in the city. People moved apartments, sometimes every year. I swear, I didn't go six months without moving at least one friend.

"Exactly."

I stole her crusts and looked around.

"It's weird seeing everything in boxes. Do you feel sad at all, leaving this place?" She shook her head.

"Definitely not. This was a place to live. Not a home. I'm looking forward to making a home with you, Lo. It's going to be so fun. I hope I don't bug you when I go and get snacks in the middle of the night. I wake up hungry all the time." I gave her a look.

"Yeah, Care, I know. It's not like I haven't been with you. Remember all those family vacations you took with us?" My parents would get a hotel room and Cara and I would get our own room and we thought we were just the most mature. We'd stay up and watch TV late into the night and order room service in the mornings and rack up a huge bill, but my parents never minded. I think they knew that things were tough for Cara at home, so they wanted to try and give her what she couldn't get there.

"Remember the time you got your period?" she said and I hid my face behind a pillow. That was one of those memories I would rather forget, and was glad only Cara and my parents knew about.

"I thought I was dying," I said. The first time I'd gotten my period had been on a trip to Disneyworld, and I had woken up with blood in my underwear and freaked Cara out by screaming and running to the bathroom. I thought I'd wounded myself or had internal bleeding. It hadn't occurred to my twelve-year-old brain that it could be my monthly cycle until Cara practically broke down the bathroom door and found me sobbing on the floor.

Once she'd explained things to me, and my mom had reminded me that we had talked about this happening plenty of times, I calmed down and then put in my first tampon and had a great day at the Magic Kingdom.

To this day, I couldn't think about how dramatic I'd been without wanting to fall through the floor.

"But you lived," Cara said, finishing her pizza and sitting next to me on the couch.

I snuggled into her shoulder.

"Somehow I did. Thanks to you." She reached over and started playing with my hair.

"We should get a bigger couch," she said. Right now I didn't have one. I'd gotten rid of the one I'd purchased at a thrift store in college when I'd moved in with Lisa. I guess I thought that since hers was better, I didn't need mine. And that by the time I needed a new couch, I was going to have enough money to buy one. I guess it wasn't a totally outlandish idea, because now I would have enough money to get a fancy couch.

"What color do you think?" she asked. I closed my eyes as she softly scratched my scalp. I was going to ask her to braid my hair before I left. Cara had a gift for doing intricate braids and it meant I didn't have to fuss with my hair for a few days.

"I'm not sure," I said, starting to get drowsy. "What do you think? I've never really decorated before. Not in an intentional way. I just pick stuff I like, even if it doesn't go together." Cara snorted.

"Yeah, I know. Do you mind if I do a little decorating? Even if you buy the stuff, I can help arrange it in the right way." I opened my eyes.

"There is a right way to decorate?" I asked. I wasn't aware of this.

"Yes, there is." She seemed really sure about that.

"Have I been decorating the wrong way?" I already knew the answer. Cara looked at the ceiling and sighed heavily.

"Okay, that's it," I said, going for that ticklish spot on her ribs. "There is no wrong way to decorate, say it!"

"Never!" Cara screamed through giggles. She tried to get away and only succeed in getting both of us onto the floor in the midst of all the boxes. Thankfully she had a thick carpet on the floor, or we might have had injuries.

She thrashed from side to side.

"Say it," said, ducking out of the way of her flailing limbs.

"You'll have to kill me," she said, and I gave up.

"Fine. Maybe you have better decorating sense than me," I said, laying on my back as she caught her breath.

"That was mean."

"It's not my fault I'm not ticklish at all. My tickle button is broken." Cara snorted. Our sides were pressed together and I wanted to reach out and take her hand. It seemed like the right thing to do, so I did. She flinched for a second, but wrapped her fingers in between mine and held my hand.

My heart did a slow happy roll, like a cat basking in a bit of sun on the floor.

"How are you going to do your hair?" she asked.

"Huh?" I said. I was too distracted by the feel of her hand in mine.

"How are you going to do your hair? I could braid it for you." she said, letting go of my hand and turning on her side to look down at me.

"Yeah, that would be great," I said, trying not to think about the way her letting go of my hand made me feel hollow inside.

"What are you going to do?" I asked.

"Not sure. Probably loose. And I kind of ordered something online. One for each of us." She blushed a little.

"What is it?" I asked, and she got up and pulled out a box that was hidden behind a stack of other boxes. It was as if the boxes had mated and kept multiplying.

"It's probably silly, but I couldn't resist. And they won't die, so we can keep them forever." She pulled out two identical bouquets, each with pink and cream flowers. They sincerely looked real. I couldn't stop myself from smelling them. Plastic.

"They're so pretty," I said, taking mine.

"I thought so. And they were on sale, so there's that." Pretty and cheap? Hell yes.

"How are we going to do this, exactly? Like, do we walk down the aisle together? Is there an aisle?" Cara blushed again.

"What?"

"So I might have looked up the courthouse and what it looks like. There is an aisle. So what do you want to do with that?" I thought about it for a few moments.

"What if we walked toward each other at the back, and then both walked down together? Then it's not like one of us is waiting for the other. We're already together when we get there." Cara beamed.

"I hoped you would say that. That's what I want. Should we practice?" I looked around, but there wasn't a whole lot of room until Cara started shoving boxes out of the way to make a small path from the living room to the kitchen.

"We need music," she said, picking up her bouquet.

"Are they going to play music?" I asked. I was sure that was on the site.

"We can. We just have to bring it with us. They can hook it up to the speakers if we have it on one of our phones. Let me know what song you might want. I can't pick. But for now, I'll just play something traditional." She fiddled with her phone and put on the traditional wedding song.

"Come here," she said, taking my arm. "Now we walk." I started forward, but she yanked me back.

"No, you have to step slow. Like this." She took one step and put her feet together and then did it again.

"Is that how we have to do it?" This was getting more complicated than I wanted it to be.

"Yes, now walk with me." I didn't feel like it, but I wanted to humor her, so I let her drag me down and then go back and then do it about ten more times.

"You know that there will be no pictures of this. And no one is going to see it but whoever is marrying us, Mom, Dad, and Ansel? And that this isn't a real wedding?" The lines kept getting blurrier and blurrier. We shouldn't have gotten dresses, probably. Or let my parents plan us a pretend reception. We should have just gotten it done and not told anyone. The rings had been the first step into making this feel more like a legit wedding and I was regretting how impulsive I'd been when I'd made us get them.

"I don't care. I want it to be right," she said, and her grip on my arm tightened. She wanted this. Walking down the aisle the way she wanted would make her happy, so I was going to fucking suck it up and do cartwheels down the aisle if that was what she wanted. I'd do anything for her. We had already sort of crossed the line of real and fake wedding, so we might as well let it ride until we got through it. Afterward, we could go back to remembering this was not a real wedding, not a real marriage, and swim in our pool full of money.

At last I walked "correctly" and Cara was happy.

"Do you want to choose a song?" I asked. Now that was something that I particularly wanted to be right. I didn't want it to just be another song like other people had. We couldn't be generic when it came to the music. I wouldn't let it happen.

"I pulled up lists, but they all seemed too traditional. This isn't traditional, so why should our song be?" she said. I scanned through a few lists, but nothing jumped out at me, so I went through my giant database of music. Nothing really said 'wedding' but did that matter? We only had to have a song that was us, and that was slow enough to walk to.

I made a quick list of five songs and made Cara listen to them.

"This one," she said as the second song started to play.

"Don't you want to hear the others?" I asked, but she shook her head.

"No, this one." It was Halsey's cover of I Walk the Line by Johnny Cash. A little melancholy, but it was one of my favorites.

"You want to practice?"

"No. I want to save it for the day," she said as the song finished.

"Sounds good," I said with a yawn. "Hey, you want to come over and stay? Lisa's gone so we can do whatever we want." I was still getting used to the fact that I was living by myself for a few days until Cara moved in. I still poked my head out of my door before I went out into the kitchen to make sure Lisa wasn't there. And then I remembered she was gone and did a little shimmy of joy. That girl really had poisoned the atmosphere in the apartment. She'd been a malignant black cloud and now she was gone, I was free and happy. It was going to be even better when Cara moved in. Everything was going to be perfect. My best friend was going to be taken care of and I wouldn't have to reuse dryer sheets. What more could you ask for?

Twelve

The morning of the wedding, I was flipping out. I hadn't slept at all, and I had dark circles under my eyes. I slathered on the makeup and put my hair in a ponytail. Cara was going to be over in a few minutes to do my hair, I was going to do her makeup, and then we were going over to the courthouse. My parents and Ansel had wanted to come over to "help prepare," but I had said no. We didn't need to make this into a bigger thing. I was already having a hard time getting my hands to stop shaking as I applied my eyeliner. I had to wipe it off and start over three times.

My doorbell rang and I dashed downstairs to let Cara in. She had a huge bag with her and I had no idea what was in it since my parents had picked up our dresses and were in charge of bringing them to the courthouse so we could change there. What did she have in there?

"So, since this isn't a real wedding and we're not doing a honeymoon or anything, I decided that I'm sleeping over." She dropped the bag in my room and joined me in the bathroom, hopping up on the sink.

"Do you want to do your hair first?" she asked.

"Yeah, sure." I turned around and took it down so she could do her thing.

"I think I'm just going to do a low messy bun, kind of like what Chloe did when I tried on the dress. I'm glad we're not doing veils. Veils are weird and have gross connotations." I agreed with her, but a little part of me kind of wanted to see what Cara would look like with one on. Not like, over her face, but maybe tucked under her hair and flowing down her back.

I stayed still as Cara combed water and mousse into my hair and then started braiding it back. The braid started on one side of my head, then she worked it around so it formed a loose crown on my head before pulling a few pieces out to make it look casual. Then she sprayed the hell out of it with spray so it would stay that way. I checked myself in the mirror and the effect was gorgeous. Ethereal and whimsical.

"Okay, your turn." I decided to go with a fresh and glowy look since her dress was pink, and pulled that color in, using it on her eyelids and to highlight her cheeks. I brushed her lips with a peachy pink lip color and then we were done. I finished my makeup and then it was time to go.

"Hey," Cara said, reaching for my arm before I left the bathroom with my makeup bag. She was still sitting on the sink and hadn't said much as I did her makeup. It wasn't like her to be so quiet, but I assumed that she was just thinking about everything. I had a million thoughts going through my head right now, and was trying to shut them up for a little while so I could focus on what we still needed to get done.

"What?" I said. "We really need to go." I normally wasn't the one who kept us on a schedule, but I guess we were reversing roles today. She would take over once we got there, I was sure of it.

"I just..." she let go of my arm and pressed her hands on the counter to lean closer to me.

"Yeah?" I said, stepping closer.

"You just look really great, that's all. And I'm really excited to be your wife, Loren." Everything stopped. I froze and couldn't stop looking at her.

She looked incredible. Honestly, I couldn't look at her or I'd get completely and totally distracted and want to spend the rest of the day staring at her instead of marrying her. I also knew that once we added the dress and the bouquet, I was definitely not going to be able to focus on anything else. She took up all the space in my head, and she was doing it now.

"You look amazing. And I can't wait to be your wife," I said in a voice that didn't sound like mine. Cara held her arms out and I walked into them. She held me tight, like she was worried I was going somewhere.

I held her back, and not just because she wasn't letting go. I didn't want to let go either. I could smell her hairspray and light perfume and just the tiniest bit of sweat. I knew I wasn't smelling all that great right now. The stress sweat was real.

I ran one of my hands up and down her back, hoping I could soothe any kind of anxiety she might have. I used to do that when we were kids. Cara would get so stressed about school projects and I would always rub her back to make her feel better. I didn't know if that would still work now, but I was going to try.

"It's going to be amazing," I said, speaking about the wedding, but I was also talking about moving in together and our life going forward. Cara was going to get everything she wanted, and I was going to see to that. I was going to be there for every step, making sure she knew she could do it, and that she deserved it. My mom's words came back to me. That we both deserved to be happy. Making Cara happy made me happy, bottom line. Honestly, even if I wasn't getting any money out of this deal, I would have done it for her. Always for her.

Cara let out a little sigh and finally ended the hug, but didn't pull away. Our faces were so close I could count every one of her eyelashes. They were so long she didn't even need extensions or falsies. I'd been jealous of them for years.

My face went hot and cold and there was a squeezing sensation in my chest that I'd never had before. Cara leaned forward just a little.

Was... was she going to kiss me?

No. Impossible. Cara was my best friend. She was also completely and totally straight. I knew her and I knew that was true. There was no question about that. I blinked and then my phone went off, scaring the shit out of both of us. I tore my eyes away from her face and looked down at my phone.

"My parents are wondering where we are." We were totally off schedule, but I didn't care anymore.

"Oh," she said, her voice a little dreamy. "Then we should probably go." I realized I needed to step away from her so she could get off the counter and leave the bathroom. I did, moving mechanically through the apartment to make sure that I wasn't forgetting anything. Not that my brain was even working. It was all muddled and fuzzy and confused.

Cara grabbed my makeup bag and a few things from her bag and we rushed downstairs to the car that had been waiting for us. I gave the driver the address of the courthouse and sat back, not looking at Cara.

"You okay?" she asked. I nodded and gave her a smile.

"Yeah, I'm just thinking about stuff. Wedding stuff." That was a good enough excuse and it wasn't that far from the truth.

"It's going to be fine. It'll be over in a few hours and then we get to go to your parent's place and have a great time."

This time she reached for my hand, but she didn't let go. Not until we got to the courthouse and got out of the car with all our shit. We found my parents in the lobby, both dressed as if they were going to a real wedding. My dad even had flowers pinned to his jacket and my mom had a corsage with pink flowers on it that almost matched our bouquets.

"Mom, I told you not to do this," I said through gritted teeth. Ansel came around the corner in his classiest pinstriped pants, black jacket, blue shirt and a light pink skinny tie.

"All of you were supposed to wear regular clothes," I said, but no one was listening to me.

"You knew we weren't going to do that, right?" Ansel said and then he looked over his shoulder and motioned to someone down the hall. "So, I know this was all secret and shit, but I couldn't keep my mouth shut." He turned back to me and gave me his adorable sheepish smile that he could use to get out of (or get into) any situation he wanted. Many a lady had been seduced by that smile.

"Yeah, I guess I should have known," I said, as at least seven more people in wedding attire came down the hall. Kell and her girlfriend Lane, Jason, Ahn, Jamie and his partner Alex, and Cedar. The gang was all here.

"We couldn't let you do this without us," Kell said, giving both of us hugs. "You tried to be sneaky, but you made a fatal mistake telling Ansel." I glared at him, but he just beamed.

"You'll be glad they're here," he said, and then we all realized that we were even more behind schedule and needed to get into our dresses ASAP. Mom, Kell, Lane, Ahn, and Cedar all came with us to "help."

Fortunately, there was a large changing room just for this purpose, but it was chaotic in there since we weren't the only people getting married today.

I was shoved into a corner as I pulled on my skirt and tried not to rip any of the lace as the top was shoved over my head by too many pairs of hands to count.

Cara was having an even harder time with her dress as the zipper wasn't going up. There was one moment of chaotic panic and then Anh got it to go up without ripping anything.

"Okay, hair," Cara said before whipping her hair into a perfect messy bun in about three seconds. My mom sprayed her with hairspray and then made us stand there so she could "get the full picture."

"Oh, girls. I'm just so happy for you." She was tearing up and I thought about rolling my eyes, but there wasn't time. We embraced and then filed out of the bathroom and dashed to check in and get our paperwork verified. From there, we went to a waiting room where someone would call us and then we'd get to have our little ceremony. Someone came and asked if we wanted traditional vows and I realized that I'd forgotten about all of that.

"We've got some," Cara said, handing the person a piece of paper. "We also have music. Ansel?" He popped up and then went with the person to help them get the song ready. We were the first ceremony of the day, so we had a little advantage of setting our stuff up without a ton of pressure.

"We got you something else," Mom said, looking at her phone and then waving someone else over.

"Are you kidding?" I said, but Cara smiled.

"You need to document this day," Mom said, leaving no room for arguments. The photographer shook our hands and introduced himself.

"Uh, we didn't really..." I started to say, but Cara was chatting with him and it seemed like they were long-lost best friends, so I shut my mouth and let him pose us for a few pictures. It was a little strange holding Cara and looking into her eyes and pretending to be romantic, but Zane, the photographer, said we were doing great and kept cracking jokes, so the both of us were laughing through every frame. At last our names were called and we walked into the room. My parents and our friends sat down in the rows of seats near the front and I tried not to drop my bouquet because my palms were so sweaty. We'd planned to walk toward each other, but that didn't work out, and they put on the song so we started walking down the aisle. I glanced at both my parents and they were both crying. Honestly.

Cara and I got to the front, and the music volume lowered as the officiant in black robes welcomed us. We joined hands without him even telling us to.

"We are gathered here today to unite Cara Margaret Simms and Loren Lynne Bowman in holy matrimony," he said, reading from an iPad.

I barely listened to the rest of his words and just kept holding Cara's hands. Mine were shaking and sweaty, but so were hers. I just kept looking at her and telling myself that we could get through this.

"Loren, would you like to share your vows with Cara?" Wait, what.

"I didn't write any," I blurted out.

"That's okay," Cara said. "Just make some up, I don't care." Well, I sure as fuck cared. This might be the only time I got to do this, and I didn't want to mess it up. Why hadn't I thought about vows until now? I guess I didn't expect to need them in this kind of ceremony.

"Oh, wow. Okay." I took a deep breath and willed my heart to stop trying to pound its way out of my chest.

"Care. You're my best friend. I love you so much and I will always love you. We're meant to be in each other's lives, as if we were created for each other. You're the only person I want to tell when something good happens to me and when something bad happens to me. You're always there for me, even when I ruin your spreadsheets." She laughed and I saw tears running down her cheeks.

"We're building a life together and there isn't anyone I would rather do that with. I love you." Cara sniffed and Ansel ran up with some tissues as she pulled a notecard out of her bra. Now it was my turn to listen to her.

"Loren. You're my best friend, and my favorite person. When my own family wasn't there for me, yours took me in. I can't imagine my life without you, and I don't want to. Whatever souls are made of, yours and mine are made of the same stuff. I love you and I can't wait to see where life takes us. Even if you ruin my spreadsheets and always make us late. I'd rather be late with you than on time with anyone else." Now I was crying. Why did she have to do that to me?

I was blubbering and crying all over the place and Cara took the tissue Ansel had given her and wiped my eyes. My makeup was probably running. I bet I was a complete mess. I was definitely going to delete these pictures.

"Cara and Loren have shared their vows with each other and all of us. Now for the second part." He turned to Cara and smiled at her. I was barely aware he was even here. All I could see was her.

"Do you, Cara Margaret Simms take Loren Lynne Bowman to be your wedded wife, your best friend and your soulmate?"

Cara threw the tissue down and took my hands again. We both laughed and cried as she said, "I do," and then it was my turn.

"I-I do," I said and the weight of what we were doing settled on my shoulders so hard that I thought I was going to fall over.

"With the power vested in me by the state of Massachusetts, I pronounce you married. You may seal your vows with a kiss."

I hadn't thought that anyone was going to be seeing this, so I figured we could just tell the officiant that we weren't going to kiss, or maybe do a fake kiss or something, but there hadn't been time. Now everyone was staring at us and we were crying and my parents were crying and Cara was looking at me as if I was the most important person in the entire world.

I opened my mouth to say something, and then Cara tugged me forward. It was either fall into her, or dive sideways and eat the gross carpet, so I fell into her, and consequently, my lips met hers. It was happening before I realized and my body seized up for half a second. Then my brain screamed OMG, YOU'RE KISSING CARA AND SHE'S KISSING YOU AND THIS IS YOUR WEDDING AND YOU'RE MARRIED NOW and kissed her back.

I kissed her back. Her lips were soft and sweet on mine, and slightly salty from our combined tears. What started as a simple pressing of our lips together quickly turned into... something.

She inhaled and sucked my bottom lip into her mouth. Oh. I trembled and held onto her desperately. Dimly, I heard people cheering, but I was completely consumed by Cara. She let go of my lip, but only to let her tongue reach out and taste me. It was gone before the sensation registered. I wobbled and almost fell over as she smiled and then we walked back down the aisle to the song My Life Would Suck Without You. I had the suspicion Ansel was responsible for that one. I was going to yell at him later, but for now, I couldn't stop smiling and holding Cara's hand.

"OKAY, THAT'S PERFECT," Zane said. Cara and I had been posing on the steps of the courthouse for the better part of an hour. He'd made us do all kinds of shots, even ones where we kissed each other on the cheek, but he hadn't pushed us to do any lip kissing, which I was grateful for. I was still off-balance from the kiss during the ceremony. Cara and I hadn't had time to talk, let alone about that.

After a few more group shots, Zane finally agreed to stop and said he would be sending us a flash drive with our pictures in a few weeks, and posting a few test shots online so we could tell him if we liked them or not.

"Great, thanks," I said.

"You're two of my favorites. I can tell you're really in love. These are going to be dynamite." I rolled my eyes at his back as he went to talk with my parents.

"I bet he says that to all the couples."

"Maybe not," Cara said, adjusting some of my hair. "I'm starving."

"Me too. Maybe we should have had a reception. Then we'd get food sooner." She nodded and then I called out to my mom.

"Are we ready to go?" She nodded, and we rounded up our friends and piled into several cars. Cara and I were stuck with my parents, and the rest split between three cars to head to the house about an hour outside of the city.

"Mom, can we stop somewhere? I think my body is going to digest itself." As if it was listening, my stomach growled.

"We're going right to the house, we'll be there soon. Can you wait?" It was like being seven again on a long car trip.

"Um, not really. And Cara is hungry too." She nodded.

"Okay, fine, we'll go through the drive thru, but you're not getting anything that might spill on those dresses. Just a quick snack to hold you over." Yup, I was a child again.

My dad found a fast food restaurant and we got in line.

"I hope this line doesn't last too long, we really need to beat everyone to the house," Mom said. She was fretting and Dad put his hand on her arm.

"It'll be fine. It's all going to work out. Don't stress." They smiled at each other and I felt some of the tension instantly ease. My parents balanced each other so well. When one of them got uptight about something, the other helped calm them down, or supported them through the storm. I'd always known that they loved each other, even if they didn't say it every day. They had the kind of relationship that I had always wanted, but didn't think I could have. That kind of love was like lightning striking the same place twice. It didn't just happen every day.

We finally got to the window and, regardless of what my mom said, Cara and I both ordered large fries with ketchup, sodas, and a double cheeseburger to share.

"You're going to ruin your appetites. I worked so hard on planning this," Mom said, but let us order.

"It's not that much, Mom, and I promise you we will be hungry again. This is just so our bodies don't eat ourselves. Because my arm is looking kind of tasty right now." My mom wasn't usually so frazzled, so I wasn't quite sure how to handle her, but Dad just laughed and handed us our bags.

"Fine, if you're going to do this, then at least let me take pictures." Cara and I posed with fries held to our faces and did another cute one where we were both taking bites out of the burger at the same time. Mom was having a coronary about us spilling, but we'd covered ourselves with napkins she'd handed us from under her seat, and there were stain-remover pens if we needed them. I wasn't worried. I was just going to eat really carefully.

"Oh my god, this is so good," Cara said through a mouthful of burger.

"Seriously," I agreed and shoved as many fries as I could into my mouth.

"Remember what we ate after our wedding?" Dad said, smiling at Mom in that special way that was reserved just for her.

"Of course. Everyone stared at us when we walked in and I remember a few asked if we were in a play and were shocked when we said we were just married. And then we got free pie," Mom said. I'd heard the story dozens of times before: they had gone to the courthouse and then to the local diner because it was one of the only decent places to eat in our small town. They'd still been wearing their wedding attire, and had even gotten dollars handed to them by patrons wishing them luck. Oh, and the free pie.

"So really, we're just continuing that tradition," I said, fishing out the last fry. Cara pouted as she realized she was out of fries. I handed mine to her.

"Here, you can have my last one." She beamed and shoved it in her mouth.

"That was quite a ceremony. I wasn't expecting to get emotional, but it happened anyway," Dad said. "I didn't know you would do vows and everything. Did you plan that?"

"Uh, not really," I said.

"I did, just in case," Cara said, wiping her hands with the napkins and shoving them back in the fast food bag.

"And why didn't you talk with me about it? I was totally thrown because I was thinking about so many other things and vows kind of slipped my mind," I said.

"I'm sorry. I kind of wanted to surprise you? And I didn't want to freak you out ahead of time, I guess. Vows seem kind of serious, don't they?" Yeah, they had felt serious. I might be panicking a little about this whole marriage thing. I knew other people had done this for all kinds of reasons, but hearing the words and signing the papers made it official. We were now legally married. We might not share each other's names, but we shared everything else. And we were going to share our money.

"Yeah, they are. But I think I did okay? Honestly, it's all kind of a blur." This whole day was a blur. When I looked back on it, I probably wasn't going to remember much. One thing I did know I would never forget was the way Cara had kissed me. She'd really gone for it, to make it convincing.

"I know," Cara said. "That's why I had to write my stuff down ahead of time. I knew my brain was going to blank. I mean, I'd practiced, but it was a whole other thing standing up there. Maybe they should have classes or something to prepare you for that stuff."

"And how to find an apartment, and pay bills and all of that." My parents laughed.

"You'll both figure it out, kids. We did," Mom said, smiling at us over her shoulder.

"I hope so." I shared a look with Cara and she smiled back at me. Holy shit, Cara was my wife.

Thirteen

We finally got to the house and Mom got out almost before the car stopped moving and headed to the barn.

"We're not just having some food in the house?" I asked Dad, but he just winked at me in the rearview and got out of the car to hold the door open for me and Cara to get out.

Our friends were standing around their cars waiting for us and they let out cheers.

"You're all dorks," I said, but I couldn't help but smile.

We all headed into the house to find that Mom had commandeered Dad and Ansel to help her do whatever it was that she was doing.

"Mom?" I asked, but she was too busy giving orders. I shrugged at Cara and we went to sit in the living room.

"This dress is so comfortable, I never want to take it off," Cara said with a sigh.

"You both look amazing, seriously. I'm more than a little jealous," Cedar said. She had a hardcore passion for fashion and also worked as a makeup artist. We probably should have asked her to come and help us, but I hadn't known that she was coming today.

"I feel like I'm probably melting. And I know my makeup is smeared," I said. Cara's eyes were smudged as well from crying. Cedar's eyes lit up.

"Can I touch you up? Or give you a new look? Please?" She never let an opportunity go by without doing our makeup. Even if we were just going out for ice cream. I never minded being her canvas.

Cara and I both sighed at the same time.

"I'll go first," she said, and then Cedar ran to the car for her kit that she always had with her in the trunk. When Cedar came back, she sat Cara down in a chair and did her magic, wiping off everything I'd done and starting fresh. I didn't mind. I sat with everyone else and talked about the wedding and that we were moving in together and how fast things changed and how adult getting married was.

"We might do it, what do you think?" Kell said, looking at Lane.

"You asking?" Lane said, putting her arm around Kell.

"I don't know. Maybe."

"Whoa, one wedding at a time," Jason said. "I can only take so many emotions."

"Let's just get through this one," I said. Cedar finished with Cara and I had to give her props for her skills. She'd done more of an evening look, accentuating Cara's eyes and giving her more of a dramatic lip.

Mom ran in and asked for more people to come help, so while Cedar finished my face, most everyone was roped into helping in the barn.

"This is going to be ridiculous," I said to Cara, who stayed with me.

"Probably. But when else can we have such an awesome party?" She had a good point. You should be allowed to have parties for all kinds of things. Parties for getting a new job, or moving, or buying a car. With presents and food and dancing. How awesome would that be?

"I'm just hoping we can relax a little. This has been the longest day ever. I'm going to sleep so good tonight."

"As long as I don't starfish and steal the whole bed," Cara said in a teasing tone.

"No way, I'm going to push you onto the floor. I need my damn sleep." She laughed and Cedar sprayed my face with finishing spray.

"There, you're golden," she said, and I checked my face. She'd done a similar look as Cara's, so we were almost matching, but she'd tailored the colors to complement our skin tones.

"Thanks, babe," I said, giving Cedar a hug. "Want to go see what kind of mayhem is happening in the barn?" I said to both of them.

"Let's go," Cara said. "Maybe there will be a bounce house? Every reception should have a bounce house."

"And a chocolate fountain," I added.

"I wouldn't mind giant beanbags for laying down. Instead of uncomfortable chairs that are wobbly and hurt my back," Cedar added.

"Beanbags are a must," I said, agreeing.

We left the house and headed over to the barn. The doors had been thrown wide and my mouth dropped open.

"Wow," I said.

"Pretty much."

"I feel like I'm in a postcard," Cedar said.

Mom had outdone herself. Strings of beautiful lights had been draped over the rafters and hung down the walls, as if it was raining drops of starlight. There were a few tables with fancy cloths on them and tons of food, and she'd even brought in speakers to play soft music. A space had also been cleared to make a dance floor.

"Is that a cake?" Cara said, pointing to the end of the food table.

"They didn't," I said, even though the evidence was right there. They got us a wedding cake with our initials on top. L and C.

"My parents are something else," I said, and that was when Mom rushed over, her cheeks flushed with excitement, and her hair flying everywhere.

"I think we're finally ready for you. Welcome to your reception that is not a reception." She waved her arm dramatically to indicate the barn.

"Mom, this is too much. You didn't have to do this. At all."

She put her arm around me and gave me a sloppy kiss on the side of my forehead.

"I know I didn't have to, but I wanted to. For both of you." Cara was tucked under her other arm and got the same kiss treatment.

"This is amazing. And you definitely didn't have to do this, but thank you," Cara said.

"Anything for my girls. Okay, let's get this started!" We all headed for the food table first and Mom had all of our favorite things: mini pizzas, spinach and artichoke dip, sushi, Reuben sliders, pickles, a huge cheese tray, and all our favorite juices and sodas.

"Look," Cara said, poking my arm as we grabbed some plates. I glanced to the other end, near the cake.

"Apple pie," I said, smiling at her.

"Apple pie promise."

Even though we'd eaten a little not long before, we were hungry again and loaded up our plates and took them to one of the tables.

"I can't see everyone," I said. I loved everyone here and I didn't want to exclude anyone.

"Can we move the tables into a square?" I asked Mom.

"Oh, sure," she said, and everyone rushed to push the four rectangular tables so they formed a square and we all sat on the outside. It was a little bit like being in a school classroom again with all our desks this way so we could have better class discussions, but it worked. I sat with Cara on my left and my parents on my right, and everyone else filled in. It was a little strange not having any family here, but neither Cara nor I was super close with our extended family, and a lot of them lived several states away and wouldn't have been able to come anyway. Plus, there was the whole "we're getting married out of the blue, wanna come?" way we'd done it. I was glad to just have these people here. Everyone I considered family, whether we were blood-related or not.

"Oh, the champagne," Mom said, getting up and rushing over to a bucket on the food table that was filled with ice and bottles of wine, beer, and apparently champagne.

"We have to have a toast," she said, filling everyone's glasses as Dad helped her.

"You don't have to do the whole toast thing," I said, trying to wave her off, but Cara put her hand on my leg under the table.

"Let her do it, Lo," she said in my ear and I decided that I should probably just shut up now and let this whole thing happen and enjoy it. No, we hadn't asked for this, but my parents and our friends had come together to support us and that was a lot more than some people had. Why couldn't I just let myself have this?

"Relax," Cara said, giving my leg a little squeeze that almost made me jump out of my chair.

I could do that. I was going to do that.

"To Loren and Cara, my daughter and now my other daughter. May you have health, wealth, happiness, and joy in your life together. We love you. Cheers!"

"Cheers!" We all said and drank.

"Do we have to make speeches?" I asked.

"No, no, we don't have to do all that. I just wanted to say a little something. Your father and I also have a little something for the two of you." Dad pulled a card out of his coat pocket and handed it to me. I grit my teeth and hoped there wasn't money in there. My parents didn't have money to give to me, and I didn't need it now. I was getting my payday next week.

I opened the card and a bunch of gift cards fell out into my lap. Cara gathered them up and I read the card. Everyone had signed it and written little notes for us. My eyes blurred with tears. Why was I crying so much today?

I passed the card to Cara and stacked up the gift cards. They were from everyone.

"Thank you all," I said, instead of scolding them for spending money on us. See? I could do this.

Cara sniffed and wiped at her eyes with her napkin.

"Seriously, thank you. This means the world that you support us." I blew my nose and Ansel called for another toast. At this rate I was going to be under the table soon. Champagne always hit me hard for some reason.

We went back to our food, which was now a little cold, but no one cared. Everyone stuffed their faces and talked and laughed and drank and I hadn't had such a good time in ages. I had a tendency to pull away from my friends sometimes, completely unintentionally, but I needed to connect with them more. Now that Cara and I were living together, we could become a sort of home base and have parties and movie nights. When I lived with Lisa, having anyone over was a crapshoot. No more passive aggressive staring as she went to the bathroom, or peering out at us from her bedroom near the living room. I never wanted to see or hear about Lisa again.

After the food, Dad got the speakers going and Ansel was in charge of the music.

"Thanks for the exit song, by the way," I said as we got up from the tables and tossed our paper and plastic utensils away.

"Yeah, I figured that would be a good one. I didn't have much time to choose. I was DJ-ing on the fly." He grinned and headed to another small table that used to sit in the yard with a few chairs that we used in the summer when the weather was nice.

"It was a great song," I said, and Cara agreed. He gave us both hugs and went to do his thing.

Cara and I shuffled our way to the dance floor, kicking off our shoes. We'd both worn ballet flats for the wedding, figuring we'd rather be comfortable and not fall down when walking down the aisle. It had been a good plan and my feet weren't killing me now. They probably would be by the end of the night. I was going to dance my ass off.

"May I have your attention," Ansel said, his voice blasting through the speakers.

"Okay, who gave him a microphone," Cara said, laughing.

"I heard that," he said, and then cleared his throat. "Since I am in charge of the music for this shindig, I have chosen a song for the couple's first dance." I looked at Cara.

"Are we doing that?" I asked her, and she nodded.

"Of course."

I'd danced with girls a few times, but never with one shorter than me. Cara giggled as we tried to figure out what to do with our arms. We ended up with one of our hands linked, and one hand on the other's back. It worked.

Ansel started the song and I smiled at Cara. Mary Lambert, "She Keeps Me Warm". How appropriate.

I started singing and Cara joined in as we swayed back and forth to the beat. Cara loved this song ever since I sent it to her a few years ago. Ansel had to know that.

Cara and I danced around until the song ended and then another started and we waved everyone to join us. Even my parents came out to groove. I tried not to cringe as my dad pulled out some of his sweet moves. I got sweaty almost immediately because the barn was stuffy and hot, but it didn't matter. I twirled Cara around and around until she stumbled from dizziness and then pulled her close. Our skin was damp and so were our dresses, but I didn't care. She pressed against me as we swayed and shimmied and made total fools of ourselves.

After a while, we were breathing hard and needed a break, so that's when my parents brought out the cake and Cara and I had to cut it and shove it in each other's faces. I almost wish we'd had a photographer for that one, but a few of our friends snapped shots on their phones.

The cake was chocolate with strawberry frosting inside for the top layer, and spice cake with cream cheese frosting on the bottom. Both of our favorites. It was almost like they knew us really well.

We both also went for pie, because my mother's was the best. She had the most perfect crust technique, so the top didn't collapse over all the apples, or puff up and leave a huge space inside.

After cake and pie there was more dancing and more drinking and carousing and so much laughter that my stomach hurt and I started losing my voice.

Cara and I crashed into two chairs next to each other and I put my head on her shoulder.

"I'm dead," I said. "Completely dead. This has been the longest day of my life."

"But one of the best?" she said, turning her head to look at me.

"Yeah, one of the best. Definitely." I lifted my head and the memory of our kiss during the wedding rushed back. I'd been pushing it aside for the entire day, but now my brain and my body were weak and couldn't hold it back anymore.

She blinked and I realized that she had glitter on one of her cheeks. I had no idea where it came from, so I reached up to brush it off, but wound up stroking her skin instead.

"You're so beautiful," I said.

"So are you." Her breath hitched in her throat and her eyes were wide.

A cough interrupted us and we both looked up to find Ansel grinning at us.

"So, we're going to wind this thing down, but would you like to do one last dance?" I was about to drop from exhaustion, but I wanted to end this night the right way. I stood up and held out my hand for Cara.

"Let's shut this shit down, Care."

Thirteen

The fee was astronomical, but neither Cara or I wanted to ride back to the city with my parents, and our friends had offered, but I was tired from all the socializing. I loved them, but they could be a lot. We were exhausted, they were exhausted, and I just wanted to chill out with her, just the two of us.

"Thank you for everything, Mom. This was amazing, and I'm glad you did it. Even if I was a pain in the ass about it before." I hugged her hard and she held me tight.

"You deserve it. You both deserve happiness and I'm so glad you liked it. Anytime you want to do another party, let me know. I think I've found my new calling." It was true, she had done a great job on short notice.

"Maybe that's a new market: last minute receptions." She laughed and went to give Cara a hug. Dad hugged me and told me that he loved me and Cara, and to come visit more often.

"I will," I said, meaning it. I had neglected them recently, and it wasn't right. Now that I had more money, I could even rent a car and come out here on the weekends with Cara. Cara, my wife. I would never get used to that, and I would never get used to the fact that I was her wife.

Our friends departed with promises to come and help us unpack next week and finally the car arrived to take us back.

"I've never been so tired in my life," Cara said through a yawn. "I was not expecting that at all. Maybe a nice dinner with your parents, but not an awesome party. That was great." She let her head fall back on the headrest and turned to give me a sleepy smile.

"It was. I never thought I wanted something like that, but now I can't imagine having this day without all of that. We should have more fun." Cara laughed a little.

"Yeah, we should. Now that we have more money, we can have more fun." It was true. Money could definitely buy you fun.

"I do and I don't want this to end," she said in a sleepy voice, her eyes shuttering.

"I know," I said, shuffling a little closer to her. Mom had put our bouquets in bags, and forced us to take leftovers so we weren't going to need to buy groceries for like a week. The car smelled like spinach and artichoke dip.

Cara made a grumpy sound and snuggled closer to me. I put my arm around her and let her pull her feet up on the seat and practically lay in my lap. My wife. My beautiful wife. We hadn't talked about when we were going to get the annulment, but it would probably happen soon. Maybe right after we got the money. I knew this feeling wasn't going to last, and it hurt to think about that. This whole thing was for show, a sham, but it sure as hell seemed real. I had a sleeping woman laying on my legs who had my ring on her hand and had signed a document saying that she was mine and I was hers. What could be more real than that?

I HATED WAKING CARA up when we got to the house, but I wasn't in a state to carry her upstairs with my noodle arms. She groaned and fussed and complained and was totally adorable the whole time so I wasn't even mad. I shoved her into bed and she fussed when I tried to tell her that she had to take the dress and her makeup off.

"You have to take it off or it will clog your pores and then you'll be upset. Just roll over and let me wipe your face, you goof." She moaned and flipped onto her back. I attacked her face with wipes as she giggled and batted at me.

"Just... stop, Care!" I scrubbed at her eyes and she whined, but I got most of it off. Now it was time for the dress.

"Roll over again. I need to get your zipper," I said. She pouted, but did it, and I pulled the zipper down.

"Now you have to sit up so I can get it off."

"This is too many steps," she said, but she sat up, holding her arms out so I could pull the straps off her arms. I tried not to look as she pushed the dress down off her hips and then kicked it off her feet.

"I'm going to hang this up so it doesn't end up crumpled on the floor," I said as she wrapped herself up in my blankets like a burrito. I hung the dress up and then pulled my skirt off. I tried to get the zipper for my top down, but it was too far up my back for me to reach.

"Care, a little help?" A pile of blankets on my bed made a grumpy sound and then her head emerged, her eyes half-closed.

"Huh?"

"Can you help me with the zipper? That's it, I promise. Then you can go back to sleep." She huffed and puffed, but her fingers found the zipper and started pulling it down. Really slow. She stopped halfway down, and I looked over my shoulder at her.

"Is everything okay?" I asked, but her eyes were glazed over. She was just staring at my back.

"Yeah," she said in a faraway voice before blinking and yanking the zipper the rest of the way down.

"Careful," I said, hoping she hadn't harmed the delicate lace. I slipped the sleeves off and stood up in just my bra and panties.

Cara wasn't going back to sleep. Cara was wide awake and staring.

I pretended not to notice. Maybe she was staring off into space or had checked out or something. Perhaps this was some high-level exhaustion.

I pulled on a long t-shirt and yanked it over my hips, not looking at Cara. I turned off the lights without asking her and got into bed.

"I'm so tired," I said, hoping she would get the hint that that meant I didn't want to talk and I just wanted to go to sleep and not think about the way she'd kissed me and the way she had been looking at me, not just now, but all day.

"Me too," she said in that same faraway voice.

"Happy wedding night," I said, trying to make a joke. Neither of us was getting laid, but I was pretty sure that wasn't uncommon for a lot of other people. You were so exhausted from everything that sex was probably the last thing on either of your minds. Made complete sense.

"Happy wedding night," Cara said, snuggling back down under the blankets. She let go of some of them so I could have some.

I lay on my back in the dark. Five seconds ago, I'd been so tired I thought I was going to fall asleep standing up and now my brain was running a marathon in circles inside my skull.

Cara made some noises beside me and turned her back to me. She was right there, but a million miles away. A little crack of the curtains let in a sliver of moonlight that caressed her back. I tried not looking, but I couldn't help myself. She was simply gorgeous. I'd never seen anyone as beautiful as Cara, and I never would. I knew other people might not think she was the prettiest girl in the world, but I did, and always would.

I shifted onto my side so if I moved a little closer we would be spooning. We had slept that way before by accident. So why was I so scared to touch her? It was like those other nights when she'd slept over and I'd been afraid.

No, it wasn't fear, exactly. It had a sharp edge of something else beyond fear. I pushed myself away from her. As far as I could get without falling off the bed. My head was getting confused and I needed to shut that shit down. This was Cara, my best friend in the whole world and my love for her was strictly a friendship love. Best friendship. Nothing romantic. Never had been. I'd been all about doing this wedding thing and now it was biting me in the ass.

I just needed to scrub myself of all this sentiment and get back to what mattered: getting her moved in and getting that money so she could put down her deposit for school. I would sleep so much better when we had that check in our hands and we could move forward with our lives. I'd worry about the annulment later.

Closing my eyes, I tried to wipe away the day, but it wasn't happening. Little moments kept popping up: the moment before Cara had kissed me, the way she held me when Zane was taking our pictures, the way she'd sung to me as we'd danced, her smile when I shoved the cake in her face.

I couldn't remember the last time I'd been this happy and content. No one could have a better wedding day than Cara and I'd had, and it wasn't even real. Best wedding ever.

So why did I feel like I was going to cry, and not from happiness?

The next day we both slept in and woke up around noon. I had finally fallen asleep, but it had been troubled and unsatisfying. After she left, I was probably going to try and nap. When I opened my eyes, I found Cara on her side, her eyes fluttering open.

"Hey," I said, not sure what to say to her.

"Good morning, newlywed." Her smile was lazy and slow and sent a shiver down my spine. She still didn't have anything but her bra and panties on and the sunlight glinted off her shoulder. The way she had the blankets tucked around her, you couldn't tell if she was wearing anything at all.

I shouldn't be thinking about Cara naked. It was both weird and wrong. Friends didn't think about their friends naked.

"Yeah, I guess we are," I said, stretching. My body was sore everywhere from all the dancing.

"I don't want to get up," I said, turning onto my back.

"Me neither. I wish we had room service, but the closest thing is getting delivery, but one of us still has to get up and get it." I sighed.

"But if we don't get delivery, then we have to make food. Making food is terrible and should be avoided." She nodded.

"You're right. Okay, I'm ordering and paying if you agree to put on pants and a shirt and get the doorbell when it rings." I turned and met her eyes.

"Deal."

We shifted closer to each other in bed, and it was hard to make sure my skin didn't touch hers. My long shirt had ridden up while I'd been sleeping, and I kept trying to pull it down so I was covered. Her thigh brushed against mine as she moved closer so we could look at brunch options on her phone. I pretended not to notice.

"I'm craving something really good. Biscuits and gravy? With bacon? And maybe some hash browns?" I was trying to follow what she was saying and keep my eyes on the phone screen, but it wasn't easy.

"Sounds good," I said. It actually did. I was ravenous and wanted something comforting and warm. Cara placed the order and then continued to scroll through her phone. I couldn't handle being in bed next to her anymore, so I got up and put on some yoga pants.

"Where are you going?" Cara asked when I opened the door.

"To pee?" I said. She looked up from her phone.

"Oh, right. I hope everything comes out okay." I stuck my tongue out at her and went to the bathroom. When I was done in there, I made a trip to the kitchen to put on some coffee for both of us. I nearly jumped out of my skin when a hand touched my shoulder.

"Hey, do you have any of the hazelnut creamer?" Cara asked as I stood there with my hand on my chest.

"You scared me," I said, catching my breath.

"Sorry," she said, and I turned to find her still just wearing her bra and panties.

"You might want to put something on. I have neighbors." I gestured to the windows that were only half-covered by curtains. They could definitely look right in if they wanted.

"So?" Cara said, shrugging one shoulder and going to the fridge.

"So do you want them to see you like that?" I asked. She pulled out the creamer and did a little twirl. I had to stop looking at her. I turned to the coffee maker and stared at that, as if staring would help the coffee get made faster.

"If they want to look, I don't care. I mean... whatever. I guess I'm old enough to not really care about modesty." Well, I sure did and I wanted her to put some damn clothes on.

At last the coffee brewed and then I was saved by the sound of the doorbell, and ran downstairs to get the food from the delivery person. I grabbed the bags and headed back up the stairs, hoping against hope that Cara would be covered.

She was back in bed sipping coffee and sighing happily.

"Food's here," I said, holding up the bags.

"Thank goodness. We ate so much food, but now I'm hungry enough to eat these blankets. Can we eat in bed? It seems like a newlywed thing to do." I didn't want to rain on her parade, and I'd give her literally anything she wanted, so I said, "great idea."

We spread the food out and I just decided I was going to do laundry after we inevitably spilled something. Biscuits and gravy wasn't exactly a clean food to eat.

Cara sat cross-legged facing me with the food between us.

"There's seven strips of bacon, wanna split them so we each have three and a half?" she asked me.

"You can have four pieces and I'll have three," I said, but Cara shook her head.

"No way. We're married now, we split everything evenly, including bacon." That made me smile. My face felt like it was cracking apart like stone.

"Well, that's definitely a marriage perk," I said, grabbing one of the pieces of bacon and shoving it into my mouth. The smoky saltiness revived me and then I attacked the biscuits, covering them with a rich layer of sausage gravy.

"I needed this," I said with my mouth full.

"Seriously," Cara said, gravy dripping down her chin. I used my thumb to wipe the gravy off her chin and then licked the excess off my finger.

She had stopped eating and was staring at me the way she had when I'd done her makeup yesterday. Had that only been a day ago? We had lived about a week's worth of days since then. At least.

"You okay?" I asked, and she just swallowed and looked down at the food.

"Yeah, fine. Just tired." A few moments ago she'd been bouncing and bubbling off the walls, so I didn't buy that. What was going on with her?

I went back to my biscuits and let it drop. I didn't want to push her. Was she regretting the wedding and the marriage? The idea that she would even regret it a little bit made me feel like I was being stabbed. I couldn't handle being one of Cara's regrets.

"You're not... having second thoughts?" I said, not meeting her eyes.

"About what? The biscuits? Ask me in an hour." She smiled and I shook my head.

"No, not the biscuits. The wedding and the marriage and everything." I didn't know what to do if she said yes. It would break me.

"Of course not. Are you? I mean, we haven't even been married for twenty-four hours." The rush of relief was so intense, I thought I was going to cry. I'd had too many emotions in the past day. I needed a break for at least a month.

"Of course not," I said.

Cara's eyes narrowed.

"Apple pie promise?"

"Apple pie promise. Speaking of that, we have apple pie. If you want some." Cara put her hand on her stomach and pouted.

"I ate too much, I think. Maybe that second biscuit was a mistake, but I couldn't let it sit there all alone. It looked so sad. So I had to eat it." Cara tossed the remains of her breakfast in the bag and I added my trash.

"That was perfect," I said, laying back. Cara stretched out next to me.

"You gonna stay dressed like that all day?" I asked.

"Why do you keep pestering me about what I'm wearing? Does it bother you? You've seen me in a bathing suit for days on end, Lo." Intellectually, I knew that a bathing suit and underwear were basically the same, but my brain also told me that underwear was so much more intimate. Personal. It had connotations that weren't about friendship.

"I know. It's fine," I said. Cara turned to the side.

"Does it bother you? I can put something on..." She started to get up and I reached out to stop her.

"No, it's fine. You can wear whatever you want, Care. It's your body and your clothes."

"Okay," she said, but she didn't sound convinced. I got up and took the trash out to the kitchen and got my second round of coffee. How was I going to deal with Cara being here all the time? Probably in her underwear. Why was this such a big deal?

"Can you pour me some more?" Cara asked, and I saw that she'd put on a baggy t-shirt that just skimmed the tops of her thighs. I glanced away as quick as I could so I wasn't staring at her exposed thighs.

"Yeah, sure. Give me your cup," I said and she set it on the counter and got more creamer.

"What are we gonna do today?" Cara said. "I mean, besides nothing."

"We can do nothing. Or we can go out and take a walk, or go to the aquarium or something." Honestly, I didn't want to leave the house, but being in such close quarters with Cara was scrambling my brain and making it hard to breathe.

"Ugh, I don't want to go anywhere. That means I have to put pants on. Do you want to just look at furniture online?" That sounded like a good plan.

"We can pick a couch," I said.

"Solid plan. And we don't have to worry about food because we have a fridge full of leftovers. Best day ever. Even if it's not a legit honeymoon." That comment snagged in my brain.

"Well, we wouldn't have a *real* honeymoon. You do know what people do on honeymoons, right?" I asked. She couldn't possibly be suggesting that we should go somewhere and... do what people did on honeymoons.

"Oh, I know. But can you imagine going somewhere and staying in a fancy hotel and everything? I can't remember the last time that happened. We were probably kids, right?" I thought back. I couldn't really remember many trips I'd taken as an adult. Just a few short ones, nothing major.

"Well, once we have the money, we can go somewhere. Where do you want to go?" I'd go anywhere with her. We'd have a good time anywhere.

"I get to pick?" Her eyes lit up the way they had yesterday. She'd been glowing and I wanted to bring that back. I wanted to make her look like that every single day.

"Sure," I said. "Pick a place and plan the whole thing and we can pay for it with the money. We can have a friendymoon." I was all over inventing new words lately.

"Oh, I'm excited now," she said, gulping her coffee down. "Something else to plan." Now her eyes were glittering in a maniacal way, and I was having regrets.

"What have I done?" I said, pretending to wail in despair.

"Mwahahaha," Cara said, pretending to do an evil laugh and failing miserably. She was too cute to be evil. Or maybe that was part of her master plan. Be so cute that no one would suspect that she was evil.

"Pretty soon we're going to have spreadsheets on the fridge and wall-papering everything. I'm doomed."

"I don't love spreadsheets *that* much," she said, but I gave her a disbelieving look.

"Okay, fine, I would live in a spreadsheet if I could."

I snorted, because it was true.

Fourteen

We spent the rest of the day arguing about where we were going to go for our trip. Turned out that I did have opinions about locations for our vacation.

"There are too many things that can kill us in Australia. No way. I am not being attacked by a giant spider-kangaroo-wombat," I said, and Cara burst out laughing.

"I hate to break it to you, but there is no such thing as a giant spider-kangaroo-wombat, and if there was, then it would be fucking adorable and awesome and I would want to take pictures with it." I groaned.

"No, Cara. No. We are not doing that." She made a huffy noise and crossed Australia off the list of places to visit.

"There are so many other places that have less things that can kill or maim us," I said.

"You know that people are hit by cars in Boston every single day, right?" I did, but that was different.

"At least those cars aren't being driven by giant poisonous spiders."

"They aren't in Australia."

"Maybe they are. How do you know? You've never been there." I grinned at her and she shoved me away and threw a pillow in my face.

"You're impossible."

"Your impossible wife," I said, emphasizing the word. I had no idea what it was about that word, but I loved the sound of it. I enjoyed saying it and thinking of myself as Cara's wife. Technically, I was. I had a shiny marriage certificate to prove it. In two weeks we needed to get a certified copy made at City Hall and then the paperwork for the withdrawal notarized. And then the money would be wired to my brand-new bank account just for that purpose, minus some that was going to a savings account for tax purposes. Fuck that. Who wanted to think about taxes? I mean, other than accountants, and maybe not even them.

"Yup, my wife. My wife who has decided that there's something wrong with an entire continent just because there might be some dangerous animals. There are dangerous animals in the US too." Now I was the one who wanted to shove a pillow in her face.

"Anywhere else. Anywhere other than Australia," I said, and she sighed heavily.

"Fine, crush my dreams."

"Isn't that *also* my job as your wife?"

"Stopppppppp."

Monday we went to my local bank to get the paperwork notarized. I wished we could get the marriage certificate, but that wasn't going to happen because of bureaucracy. I just wanted my damn money.

I took our wedding dresses to a shop to be cleaned and preserved. Who knew if either one of us was going to wear them again, but they were special dresses and I didn't want them to be stained and stinky forever.

I got some more job rejections and had another interview, but the company was a little too hardcore about pushing sales and memberships and even if they'd given me an offer, I wouldn't have accepted. Plus, the pay was crap.

"No one wants to employ me," I said, resting my head on my arm. Cara and I were out with Kell and Lane as sort of a double date. Sort of.

"You just need to find the right place. All you need is one to give you a chance." Well, that wasn't happening yet.

"It'll be fine. You'll find something. Have you thought about maybe volunteering somewhere that could potentially turn into a job?" Cara said.

"Like where?" Honestly, I was up for suggestions. In my mind, I knew that I could live on the inheritance money for a while if I needed to, but the idea of not having a job and a steady source of income, even with the extra money, made me feel like I was going to break out in hives.

"A library maybe?" she said.

"I could try that. I've also thought about maybe getting something that's more part time, so if I did that, then I could still work at a job. The idea of anything other than full time terrifies me." I wasn't going to blow this.

"That sounds like a good idea," Cara said, brushing my shoulder with her fingers. She'd been doing that a lot lately. Or maybe I was just noticing it now? I wasn't sure. It definitely seemed like she was taking more opportunities to touch me.

"Seriously, really smart," Lane said. "I'm not sure if I'd do that if I got a pile of money. I'd probably blow it all on bags." Lane had an entire closet just for her purses, including many that were vintage and probably worth some dough. Right now she had a designer bag slung over the back of her chair that I didn't need to look up to know it was expensive. The purple of the bag almost matched the purple streaks in her dark hair that she'd recently added. Lane also had an obsession with dying her hair any and all colors.

"If you had to save your purses or me from a fire, you'd pick the purses," Kell said, pouting.

"Oh, babe. You can rescue yourself. The purses can't. They don't have legs, or a way to carry themselves. They're helpless." She cradled her bag like a baby in her arms.

"You see what I have to deal with?" Kell said, gesturing to Lane, who was now cooing endearments to the bag. "How is marriage going so far for you two?"

We were still keeping up the pretense that we were a real couple, and it was less difficult than I expected.

"I don't know, Care, what do you think?" I said, putting my arm around her.

"It's pretty great so far," she said, leaning into me.

"I can't believe you're really together, this is so wild," Kell said, and Lane put her bag back on the chair to stop Kell's long red hair from getting dragged through her plate of spaghetti. Kell was always ending up with food in her hair or on her shirt. She carried extra clothes and detergent pens in her bag at all times.

"Is it?" I asked. Lying to my friends did make my gut twist with guilt. But they'd jumped on board with everything so quickly, that it almost didn't feel like lying sometimes.

"Yeah, I mean, you're best friends and then you say you're getting married. With like, no dating step in between." I looked at Cara and shifted in my chair.

"Yeah, well, we just decided it was right, you know?" Cara said. "And it just worked out. I know I'm not impulsive, but when Lo said she wanted to get married, I couldn't dream of saying no." She did that thing where she put her hand on my thigh under the table. She'd been doing that a lot more, I was sure of it.

"Well, I did do a perfect proposal," I said, grinning back at her.

"Yes, you did," she said, leaning closer. The noise in the restaurant faded and everything about Cara sharpened. Her eyes that were sparkling with our shared amusement. Her warm hand, which was still on my leg. The brightness of her cheeks because she'd had a few drinks. Her scent that I could pick out, even in this crowded restaurant filled with so many other smells. I could find her even in a sea of other people. I would always find my best friend.

"Tell us the story," Lane said. "I haven't heard it yet."

Cara and I took turns telling first my proposal story and then hers and flashed our rings again and talked about where we were going to go on a trip and how we thought living together was going to work out.

"Honestly, when we moved in together, I was freaking out, but it was such an easy transition," Kell said. She and Lane had been together for four years and I was surprised they weren't married yet. They were one of the first queer couples I'd met in Boston, and they'd been my inspiration for what a good queer relationship could be.

"Except for the time when we fought about what to put on the walls. And where to put it," Lane said with a smirk.

"You just didn't understand my theme," Kell said to her, and I snorted.

"Was your theme clutter? Because that's what it looked like," Lane fired back.

"Oh, unlike your collection of teapots? Because that looked pretty cluttered to me."

"You *love* my teapots," Lane said, leaning closer. It was like Cara and I had disappeared and Kell and Lane were in their own world. That was what I wanted.

"Ugh, I guess. I kinda love you too," Kell said, leaning only a few inches away from Lane's face.

"Oh you do, do you?" Lane said, smiling.

"Yeah, I do." They shared a sweet kiss and it made my chest ache. I was so happy for them, and supported them, but seeing that when I didn't have it and wanted it so much was rough sometimes.

"Hey," Cara whispered as the waitress came to ask how everything was going and if we wanted drink refills.

"What?" I whispered back.

"Are you okay?" she said softly.

"Yeah, fine."

"You sure?" I nodded and ordered another Coke.

"I'm fine."

Pretending to be married was fun most of the time, and then there were the moments when melancholy and jealousy would creep in through the back door of my mind and take up residence at the front of my thoughts.

It wasn't Cara's fault that we weren't really in love, and it wasn't her fault that I had come up with this ridiculous plan in the first place. It wasn't anyone's fault but mine. My one consolation was that it would be over soon and we could hopefully go back to being best friends. We'd been through so much already and our friendship had survived. So why wouldn't we make it through one little fake marriage?

Fifteen

"When did you get so much stuff?" I said, looking around our living room. Well, what used to be our living room before it had been infested by a plague of boxes that were stacked nearly to the ceiling.

"I'm not really sure. It doesn't seem like a lot, but then you put it in a box, and I think it multiplies." Cara said, panting a little from walking up the stairs. The movers had left and now it was up to us, and the friends that would be here in an hour, to get all this shit from boxes to not boxes.

Then there was the added complication of having to put all of her bedroom items in my room, since, you know, we were a couple and getting married. It would be strange if we didn't share a bedroom. Later, we would move everything back to her room ourselves.

"Where do we even start?" I said, starting to panic.

"Lo, it's fine. I have a system. I color-coded and labeled everything." She pulled a folded piece of paper from her back pocket.

"She has a spreadsheet, everyone," I said, and she smacked me in the shoulder with said spreadsheet.

"Who are you talking to?" she said, unfolding the spreadsheet and glancing at it.

"No one," I said as the doorbell rang. I almost tripped and died about three times before I made it downstairs to get the door open to find Ansel, Jason, Anh, Jamie and Cedar.

"Our bodies are yours," Jason said, spreading his arms out.

"What the hell are you wearing?" His outfit consisted of a blue polo shirt and black yoga pants, but the real oddity was the sweatband on his head.

"These are my moving clothes," he said, looking down.

"Fair enough." Everyone else piled into the house.

"I brought candy," Ansel said, holding up a bag.

"I didn't know we were supposed to bring anything," Jamie said. "I would have brought something if I'd known I was supposed to."

"No, no, we didn't need anyone to bring anything. Other than themselves," I said, hoping to stop Jamie from panicking. He had a hard time in social situations if he didn't know what the expectations were ahead of time.

"Okay, good," he said, leaning against a box. "Don't scare me like that, Ansel."

Ansel looked sheepish and held up the bag.

"Chocolate?"

"Absolutely," Jamie said, sticking his hand in the bag and then noisily unwrapping one of the candy bars he unearthed.

"So I've assigned you all certain rooms that I'm calling zones," Cara said, and we all looked at each other.

"Care, we don't have to –"

"Ansel, you are red, which is the kitchen zone," she continued without even noticing me, "Anh, you're blue, bathroom zone, Jamie and Cedar, you are yellow which is bedroom zone, Jason, you are green, which is living room zone." We all saluted her.

"And what about me?" I asked, a little sad to not be assigned a zone.

"You're green with Jason," she said, not looking up from her spreadsheet. I needed to get her a clipboard one of these days. She definitely needed a clipboard.

"And you?" I asked, and she finally looked up.

"I'm head supervisor," she said, flipping her ponytail over her shoulder.

"Oh, are you now?" I said.

"Damn right. Who else is gonna manage this mess?" As if they'd heard her, there was the sound of a box being dropped none to gently on the floor in another room and a loud "ooops" that followed.

"Remind me why we invited them over?" she said as she dashed off to see what had happened.

"Because we needed the help?" I called after her, but she didn't hear me.

"Hey, Jason, you ready?" He flexed and let out a grunt.

"Let's do this," he said in his Batman voice.

"Please don't do the voice. I can't take you seriously when you do the voice," I said as we looked at the array of boxes.

"You just don't appreciate the voice," he said in his regular voice.

"Okay, we need to get started or else Cara is going to come back in here and crack the whip." Jason sighed.

"I'm guessing not in the fun way." I snorted and bent down to read what was written on the closest box to me in Cara's immaculate penmanship.

"No, probably not," I said. I didn't want to think about Cara and whips in that way. It was too weird.

"Okay, this one is blue," I said, trying to pick it up, finding it far too heavy. "Jesus, what does she have in here?"

Jason closed his green eyes and put his hand on the box, and then froze, as if he was trying to listen or something.

"I'm going to say books? I'm feeling books. Definitely a books vibe," he said, nodding.

"You are such a dork, but could you lift that for me?" I asked. Jason was a total doll, good-looking as hell, and nice on top of it. If I liked men even a little bit, I would want to date him.

"Of course," he said, easily hauling the box into his arms and taking it back to the bedroom. Cara was in the kitchen with Ansel and they were definitely having a debate about something. Good grief, they were quite the pair sometimes. They only ever pretended to fight and never actually fought. More often than not, one of their fake fights ended when they both started laughing at the same time.

I went for another box and found another for the blue zone, but this one had sheets and pillows in it, so I was able to move that one myself.

Under Cara's watchful eye, we got the everything out of boxes, and in their proper places in less than three hours.

"You have a lot of stuff," I said, looking around the living room. True, it had been just about empty when Lisa had left, but I didn't remember seeing all this stuff in Cara's tiny apartment.

"I had to put a lot of this stuff in the basement because I couldn't fit it in the apartment," she said. Uh, I hadn't known about that. No wonder she had so much stuff.

"You little sneak," I said, poking her shoulder.

"Hey! You had the room, and my stuff is really nice." She was right. Most of my decorating style was "Ikea Chic" or had come from yard sales and thrift stores. Cara had actually shopped at antique stores and the kinds of places that had home furnishings. I'd never even been into one of those places.

"We still need a couch," I said, staring at the very empty space where a couch should be.

"And a coffee table, a few side tables, another chair, and some better curtains and we'll be in business," Cara said.

"Oh, is that all?" That wasn't one or two things.

"I don't think that's a lot." I made a sputtering noise.

"Aw, you two are the cutest couple. I'm so glad you're married," Cedar said. "I wish you had a show so I could just watch you together all the time."

"Little creepy, Cedar," Ansel said.

"Why is it creepy to be happy for my friends?" That sparked a long discussion about reality TV and whether real people were actors and then privacy in the internet age and then that somehow evolved into discussing whether we would want to know what thoughts animals were thinking if we could.

Ansel passed around the candy, and it was gone pretty quickly.

"Well, I feel like we owe you all food, so who wants pizza, and what kind?" Before anyone could say anything, Cara stood up from where we'd been lounging on the floor.

"Freeze. No one say anything until I write this down." She whipped her phone out of her back pocket and then turned to me.

"What do you want, Lo?"

"Mozzarella sticks. And pepperoni." Cara nodded and took that down, pivoting to face Cedar. She went around the room and figured out how to order pizzas with who wanted what, sometimes just on half, and enough appetizers to go around, and drinks. And then she split the bill so I could send her the exact amount, since we'd agreed to share the cost.

"You should just get beanbags," Cedar said, leaning against the wall.

"Maybe," Cara said in a way that meant we were definitely not even fucking considering beanbags as suitable for our living room.

"I didn't know you were such a decorating dictator. I'm learning so many things about you now that we're married," I said as she sat down after putting in the pizza order and rested her head on my shoulder.

"And you're going to learn so many more. Good and bad." I knew she was going to figure out things about me that I might have hid from her, sometimes without even intending to. You could never really know someone fully until you'd lived with them and had seen what was under the veneer they showed the world. I'd seen what was under Lisa's veneer and it was pretty rotten underneath. I was so glad to be rid of her, even if it meant that Cara had taken over the entire apartment. I still had my room to myself. She wouldn't go in and decorate it when I wasn't home. Would she? Surely not.

"You're making me want to get married," Cedar said with a dreamy sigh. "And I never thought I could get married."

"Why not?" I asked.

She shrugged one shoulder.

"I don't know. Just didn't think it was for me." Cedar didn't talk a lot about her life before she moved to Boston to go to school for makeup. I'd known her for years, but still, she didn't like to talk about her past, so I let it go. If she didn't want to talk about it, she didn't have to. Cara was the same way. When people asked about her parents, she shut right up and then ran away from the conversation as quickly as she could.

"My parents only got married for financial reasons, so I never really saw marriage as anything romantic. Huh," I said, just now realizing that.

"Well, you two are sure as hell romantic," Jason said. "You're so cute my teeth are hurting."

I blushed and Cara removed her head from my shoulder. We kept getting comments like that, so we must be fooling everyone. I glanced at Ansel, but he was fiddling on his phone.

The pizza finally arrived and we gorged ourselves until we could barely move.

"Okay, this has been a long day," Jamie said. "I love you all, but I need to go home and not be around people for a while." He got up and took care of his trash and then headed out. Everyone else but Ansel trickled out after him.

"You're still going with lying to everyone, huh," he said as we cleared up the last of the pizza mess.

"I mean, what are we going to say? We got married for money? Surprise, I had inheritance money all the time? I don't want them to know," I said. I couldn't tell him the real reason I didn't want to tell everyone: I didn't want them to think less of me.

"You know they wouldn't judge you. If they were in your shoes, they would do the same fucking thing in a heartbeat." I glanced at Cara, but she was definitely avoiding looking at me.

"It's just complicated, Ansel. I have my reasons and Cara does too."

"Well, I supported it at first, but honestly, I think you need to tell everyone. I won't betray your trust, because that would be a dick move, but I really think you should tell everyone. At least after you get your annulment. People are going to wonder. Plus, they're also going to wonder when you suddenly have a ton of money. I think you're underestimating what they're going to notice and not notice." Shit, I hadn't really thought about that. I guess I just assumed we could play this off, get the annulment and then sort of... not tell anyone and then we could break up but remain friends. Obviously moving in together changed all of that, but the plan could still work. This could still happen without telling our friends we were both greedy gold diggers.

"I can always tell them that I inherited the money and Cara got financial aid. We don't owe anyone explanations, Ansel." Cara was still quiet and I kind of wished she would jump in and defend me. She was my best friend and fake wife, after all.

Ansel sighed and put his hands up in surrender.

"I know, I know. I'm not trying to be an asshole, I swear. I just think you should give your friends a little more credit than you are right now."

I probably should, but I'd chosen this path and Cara had agreed to it with me and I wasn't going to change things up on her, unless she decided that she wanted to. I stole a glance at her, but she was looking at the floor.

Ansel gave us both hugs, and after he left, things were a little weird.

"What do you think? About what he said," I asked her after several minutes of silence.

"I don't know, Lo. I really thought the best thing was not to tell everyone, but now it feels like we're putting on a show, and I don't like it. I don't like pretending to be really married. It's dishonest, Lo." Of course it was, but that was the price we were paying for getting the money.

"So are you saying that you want to tell them? What do you think the reaction is going to be?" I had no idea how that would go, and I didn't particularly want to find out. This plan had been fine so far, with just the side effect of some guilt, but I just didn't want to see my friend's faces when we told them that this was all a lie for money.

"I don't know, Lo. I just... I don't know." She got up and walked back to her room and shut the door. This was the most tension we'd had in ages and it made me completely sick to my stomach. This had been the longest fucking day and part of me just wanted to go into my room, watch something frivolous, and go to bed, but I couldn't leave things this way with Cara.

So I crossed the room and knocked softly on her door.

"Care?" I heard her turn off her music.

"Yeah?" she said.

"Can we talk?" She was silent for a few moments.

"Yeah," she said, opening the door.

"If you want to tell everyone, I support you. It just seems like things were going fine and you suddenly changed your mind." I had missed any signs that she was uncomfortable with everything.

She stood back to let me in her room and then flopped on her bed.

"I just don't know. I feel like I never know if I'm doing the right thing. Do you ever feel that way?" She squinted at me as I sat down beside her, leaning against her mountain of pillows.

"Uh, all the fucking time. You're not the only one that feels that way. I'm pretty sure everyone does, Care." She huffed.

"Well, I don't like it. I want to know what the right thing is and then do that thing. Preferably plan out the next five things in a row and then do those things as well." I smiled. Cara and her planning.

"I mean, you could do that, but life tends to ignore plans. And sometimes your plans no longer work, so you have to make new plans. Like fake marrying your best friend so you don't end up on the street." She laughed at that one.

"I guess you're right. We can stick with the plan, but I do get moments of intense guilt. Sometimes I wish I didn't care about things as much. If I didn't care, this would be so much easier."

Story of my life. I cared far too much about all the wrong things, and didn't care about the right things. Well, except for Cara. Caring about her was the most right thing I had ever done or would ever do.

"It'll be different when the money gets here. Then you're going to be so busy with school that you're not going to have time to worry about that stuff. And I'll be doing... whatever I end up doing with my time. I haven't decided yet. I need you to help me make a list." I swear, I couldn't make a huge decision (even an impulsive one) without her input.

"I can help you make a list. Might take my mind off things."

"Yeah?" In response she pulled out one of her myriad notebooks and a pen. Cara lived for notebooks. She had dozens and dozens of them, all filled with lists and ideas and schedules and things she'd done. They were almost a form of journal for her, and she kept them all, going back to when she was a kid and scribbled her lists in crayon and colored pencil and did doodles of flowers and faces.

"Okay, hit me with what you might want to do."

We spent the rest of the evening making a progressively more silly list of potential jobs or hobbies for me to try.

"Why don't I just sit around wearing lots of scarves and drinking tea and reading too many novels?" I said.

"I mean, you can. What about becoming a book blogger? You don't get paid, but you get to read books, and that's almost the same thing."

"Put it on the list," I said.

I ended up falling asleep on her bed and waking up in the middle of the night, too tired to go back to my own. Cara hummed in her sleep and snuggled closer.

We were going to make it. We were going to be fine, I knew it. Even if we kept one tiny secret from our friends.

Sixteen

The two weeks of waiting until we could get the certified copy of the marriage certificate were both annoying and a hell of a lot of fun. Cara and I settled into a routine where she would go to work, I would go on job interviews and putter around the house and make dinner for her to come home to. We also hung out with our friends as a couple, and picked out all the new furniture we wanted to get when the money came in.

It was all adorable and domestic, and made me feel like a real wife. I even got myself a frilly apron.

"How was your day, dear?" I asked one night when Cara came home from work. I was in the kitchen with a spatula in my hand and a steak stir-fry going on the stove in a wok.

"Good, thanks," Cara said. She always seemed surprised to come home and find me in the kitchen making dinner, even though I'd been doing it consistently.

"I got another interview. This time at the Museum of Fine Arts for the gift shop. It's only part time, but I'd get a free membership, so that would be cool. We could go and be all artsy and make serious faces and comments about abstract art like we actually understand it." Cara put her chin on my shoulder from behind and put her arms around my waist. I froze for a second. Cara was definitely more comfortable with touching me now, and it wasn't my imagination. She had no problem with hugs and lying next to each other on one of our beds, or cuddling on the couch. It wasn't a big deal, but sometimes my brain told me it was.

"Sounds like fun. Plus, you'd be working with a lot of smart people and you'd get to see a lot of art. That wouldn't be bad." I didn't think so.

"Something tells me it's not going to help with my non-existent artistic talent. Oh, I need your help looking up some famous paintings so I can gush about them in the interview. That's one of the requirements." I could think of paintings that I liked all day long with no pressure, but in the intense and anxiety-provoking environment of a job interview, my brain liked to stop working. I had the rest of the questions down, but that was a new one I hadn't practiced yet.

"Of course. Hey, can you do laundry tomorrow? I really want to wear that new romper I got."

"No problem," I said, flipping some of the steak pieces in the wok with the spatula. Cara's hands were still lingering on my waist and I could feel her breath stirring my hair.

I kept moving, pretending I didn't notice that she was still there, but my lungs were struggling to work, and I didn't know how to get my brain to focus on just stirring the food.

"I can't wait to get back to school. Is that weird? I miss homework." She stepped away at last and I nearly gasped in relief. My body just went haywire whenever she was that close. I couldn't put my finger on it, but the intensity of my reaction hadn't gone down at all. It had gotten worse since we'd moved in. Our proximity was hard sometimes. It filled me with the most uncomfortable ache that made my skin and bones hurt. It never lasted very long, but the episodes had gotten more and more frequent and I didn't know how to deal with them. I just wanted to live with Cara and for everything to be fine. It was going to be fine.

"You ready for next week?" Obviously, we couldn't get our money on the weekend, so we were probably getting it sometime next week, after the financial advisor got our Priority Mailed documents. I had this horrible fear that they'd somehow get lost in the mail so I'd checked and double and triple checked the address and the name of the person processing it. Even Cara told me I was going overboard with making sure that everything was prefect. I just couldn't fuck this up. My bank account was almost empty, my car had been sitting useless in the garage, and I had bills coming up that I couldn't pay on my own. Being broke was terrifying. I was still expecting something to go wrong, or for this all to fall apart.

"I just want this all to be over. The money part, I mean. The fake marriage part is pretty great." I peeked at her as she went to the fridge to get some drinks.

"It's been good practice. Although I'm not sure what it says that I'm the only one working and you're the one here cleaning and cooking and all that." I turned around to face her.

"What's wrong with that? I'm not working right now. The least I can do is stuff around here while you're at work. And it's not like we're sharing money. All the money you have is yours." I didn't expect any sort of money from her, even if she had a repayment plan and was insisting on starting it as soon as she graduated.

"I don't know. You're already giving me all this money and you let me move in and everything. I feel like I'm mooching."

"Cara Lynne, we have already been over this, time and time again. You're not going to convince me that you're an evil moocher, so stop it." I pointed my spatula at her to emphasize my words.

She popped the top of her soda and sipped silently.

"I can't help the way I feel, Loren," she said. "The little voice in my head likes to whisper mean things to me sometimes."

"Fuck the little voice. The little voice is an asshole who should mind their own business." I would punch the little voice if I could.

"Thanks, Lo," she said, setting down her soda and opening her arms to me. I walked into them and snuggled against her. I loved the way her hair smelled and was always so shiny and silky. Mine was always a hot frizzy mess, no matter what the weather. It was especially horrible in the humidity, like right now.

I let myself hold her until I remembered the food and turned off the heat just in time so nothing burned. Cara got out plates and we went to her bedroom to eat. We'd also decided to buy a small table and chairs to eat at. No idea where we were going to put them, but Cara was going to do apartment Tetris and make it work.

My parents called pretty frequently to check up on us and see how we were doing. They'd cleaned up the barn, returned the rented tables, and Dad had coiled all the twinkle lights back up and stored them in the attic. I had no idea what else they were going to use them for, but I had the sneaking suspicion that Christmas was going to be especially lit this year. I couldn't even think that far forward. All I could think about was getting to the money, and I'd deal with everything else that came after that. I would breathe free when my bills were paid, my car was fixed, and Cara's check to pay for school had cleared. Life was going to be a cakewalk after that. Soon. We would be there so soon.

"KISS FOR LUCK," CARA said as we stared at the envelope that had all the documents required to disburse the inheritance money.

I kissed it, and then she kissed it and we headed into the post office to mail it.

"We definitely need to celebrate this one," Cara said. "I'll treat you to lunch."

I couldn't stop shaking with the stress of mailing that damn thing. Those papers were going to haunt me in my sleep. Not to mention the fact that I had my interview in a little while at the Museum of Fine Arts and I was nervous about that as well. I'd been through plenty of interviews, but this one I really wanted to nail because I thought this job wouldn't totally suck ass.

"I'm too nervous to eat," I said, shaking my head. "But I'll come with you if you want to get something."

"No, that's okay. Would you be up for getting a green juice or something?" I could handle liquids, so I agreed and we headed for the nearest fresh juice bar. We didn't have to walk too far, which was nice.

"Do you want me to come with you to your interview? I know I won't come in with you or anything because that would be weird, but I could at least drop you off and then wait for you. Maybe even browse a little."

I shook my head.

"That would be weird. Like, here I am with someone else because I'm not enough of a big girl to do this on my own." Cara sipped her mango and strawberry smoothie.

"I could pretend I don't even know you and just happened to walk into the museum at the same time. And then we can meet back up in the lobby. No one will know." The idea of knowing that Cara was waiting for me to get out of my interview did have its appeal.

"Okay, fine. But you really have to pretend that you don't know me."

"I've got this."

IN BETWEEN WAITING to hear about how the interview went, and refreshing my bank account details, I was a ball of stress for the next two days.

"We've got money!" I screamed as my bank account suddenly had more money in it than I knew what to do with. Cara ran into the living room, her toothbrush still in her mouth and toothpaste dripping down her chin.

"Seriously?" she said, spitting toothpaste everywhere. I couldn't give less of a fuck.

"Yes! It's finally here!" I jumped up from the couch and Cara threw her toothbrush on the floor and we screamed and jumped up and down and hugged each other and got coated in minty toothpaste.

She started crying and then I started crying as we just swayed and held each other.

"It's all happening, Care. It's all for you," I whispered. "I'd do anything for you."

I looked down into her sparkling eyes and it was like looking at her during our wedding all over again. She had that same gleam of happiness shining out of her so bright, she was luminous.

"I'd do anything for you, Loren," she said in a voice that was barely a whisper. One minute I was staring at her, and the next, I was kissing her minty mouth. The contact only lasted about half a second, because I pulled away so fast I almost fell over, but it was still a kiss.

"Sorry," I said, wiping my mouth with my hand. "I don't..." I let the sentence trail off and drop. I didn't know how to finish it.

"It's okay," she said in that faraway voice.

"We should probably, um, clean up?" I made it sound like a question. My brain wasn't exactly firing properly right now. It was doing its best, but everything was shaken up and scrambled.

"Right," she said, looking down at the splatters of white all over the floor and all over both of us.

"I'll... get something." I couldn't even form a full sentence without a huge pause to figure out what words were supposed to come next. I needed to do something, so I found some paper towels and cleaner and went back into the living room. Cara was picking up her toothbrush from the floor slowly. I went to work on the floor and she went back to the bathroom and I heard the sink turn on.

What the fuck was I doing? I had kissed her. What the hell? I was going to blame it on money euphoria. She'd kissed me during the wedding, so it wasn't like I was the only one doing any kissing. The toothpaste burned my lips and I wiped it off as best I could.

Cara was in the bathroom for a long time, and when she came out, I didn't know what to say, so I didn't say anything and she asked me if we could put in the order for the new furniture, so I said yes and that was that.

Money made you do all kinds of strange things. Like kiss your fake wife. I hoped it didn't change me too much. I wasn't going to let it. And I wasn't going to let myself kiss Cara again. Definitely not.

Fortunately, I got an email that distracted me (a little bit) from the spontaneous kiss.

"I got the job!" I screamed, and Cara dashed out of her bedroom in a new outfit.

"The one at the MFA?" she asked. I nodded and she hugged me again, but she let me go quickly, and stepped away, folding her hands behind her back.

"This calls for... something. Something special." We'd been celebrating so much lately that I didn't know if I could handle much more.

"Can we just order sushi and watch that new episode of the baking show in our pajamas?" I asked. That sounded perfectly celebratory to me.

Cara laughed and I hoped we'd put the kiss thing behind us and never mention it again.

"Yeah, we can do that. Solid plan."

This was going to be the best fucking sushi of my whole life.

Seventeen

My parents were ecstatic that I had the money finally, and encouraged me to use it and be practical, but also to buy myself something nice.

"I'm getting Cara this purse she's wanted for ages." I was literally on my laptop ordering it while I was talking to them.

"But get something for yourself, Loren. Something frivolous and fun," my mom said. "You deserve to have fun after working so hard for so long." I promised her that I would find something like that to spend a little of the money on. They also recommended that I find someone who could help me invest a little of the money, for tax purposes, and also for the future. I guess I was going to find out what the fuck an IRA was at last.

I asked Cara to give me a ballpark of how much money she would need, and she gave it to me exactly, right down to the cents. I glanced at the number and then added a bunch to it before I transferred the amount to her bank account.

She got the notification of a deposit on her phone and her mouth dropped open.

"Loren. What did you do?"

"I gave you more money. For books and incidentals and shit. You're going to need fancy clothes for your fancy school. And like, scrubs and so forth. I don't know anything about grad school, obviously. I just know you need a lot of money for a lot of stuff."

Cara shook her head.

"I'm transferring the extra right back," she said, but I was quick and snatched the phone out of her hand.

"I don't think so." I held the phone out of reach.

"Lo, you can't let me have that much money. I'll never pay you back." I shrugged, still holding the phone out of reach.

"So? I didn't want you to pay me back in the first place. That was your idea. I'm happy to give you most of it. I probably should have given you more." She shook her head and sighed. I hoped that was a sigh of defeat. She could transfer the money back, but I would just put it in her account again. I wasn't going to let this go.

"I'm stubborn as fuck, Care. You know you can't win." I smirked and she held her hand out for the phone.

"I really shouldn't let you do this," she said.

"But you're going to because I'm so cute and persuasive." She rolled her eyes to the ceiling.

"Why are you like this?"

"Because?" I handed her the phone back, but I was instantly ready to go for it again if she tried to trick me and send the money back.

"You're keeping that damn money and you're going to use it to get through school and then you're gonna be the best damn PA the world has ever seen and I will have the honor of being your best friend. That's more than enough for me."

Cara was trying not to smile.

"Sometimes I don't know what to do with you, Lo."

I almost blurted out something completely inappropriate about things she could do with me.

I seriously needed to get my shit together. This whole marriage thing had messed with my head, and I was acting like we were a real couple. I had to stop doing that. At least I'd managed to stop myself before I said something I would regret. Unlike that kiss the other day. We still hadn't talked about it, and I hoped we never would. I wanted to push that so far aside that I forgot that it even happened and it vanished from my consciousness. That would be great, to have a nice little memory eraser to get rid of the things you definitely did not want to think about anymore.

"Just get me a nice card. One of the ones that costs like eight dollars. Then we're even." She snorted and got up from her bed. We were still waiting for our couch, so we usually ended up in her room when we hung out since her bed was bigger than mine.

"I can't believe it's all happening. The money and moving in and all that. My brain can't catch up that this is all reality and it's happening to me. You made that possible and I can never thank you." Oh, here we go again.

I got up and put my arms around her shoulders.

"You don't have to thank me. You would have done the same, and that's all I need to know." I thought I could feel her heart racing, so I let go, but she grabbed my arm and pulled me into a hug.

"You're everything to me, Loren. I'm so glad you're my best friend."

"And fake wife," I said.

"And that." Her voice cracked a little bit, and I thought that she might be crying. I hoped they were tears of happiness. This money solved so many problems for us. Not all of them, but a hell of a lot of them.

"I love you so much, Lo," she said into my shirt.

"I love *you* so much, Care." She was definitely crying and I wasn't sure what to say to make it better, so I just did what I usually did. I held her tight and let her have a moment. When she was ready to talk (or not), she knew I was there. I'd never thought I was super good at emotional support, but I guess I'd done well enough with Cara because she was still here.

Cara stayed in my arms for what felt like ages, and I didn't think she was crying anymore, but I guess she still wanted to be held, so I was going to hold her. Forever, if I had to. I'd taken vows, after all, even if we were going to annul them. Yeah, I didn't want to think about that.

I felt her let out a huge breath and then she let go of me.

"Thanks," she said, her eyes and cheeks a little red.

"Is everything okay?" I asked.

She nodded and wiped her cheeks.

"Just overwhelmed, I guess. With everything. This has been a really busy month." It had, and I didn't want to stop and think about it. Too much had happened and there was no use going back and overthinking it now.

"It's going to be really busy when you're in school. I'm probably never going to see you. I'll be here and you'll just live in the library and your room and coffee shops and only come up for air and food and showers."

"You'll be there to make sure I eat and don't get too stinky," she said.

"Yup, that is one of my best friend duties." I saluted her and she laughed before reaching for a tissue to blow her nose.

Something hung in the air, something unsaid. I had sensed its presence ever since before the wedding, and I wasn't sure what to make of it. These few weeks had been some of the happiest and most confusing of my life so far.

"Do you ever feel like... like you don't know yourself as well as you thought you did?" Whoa, that was some deep shit. I needed to sit down for this. I claimed my spot on her bed and patted the spot next to me. She sat down and I could tell from the wrinkles on her forehead that she was wrestling with something.

"What do you mean?"

She fiddled with the edge of her blanket, twisting and untwisting it.

"I'm not sure. I guess I'm just having this feeling that something has changed and I don't know what it is, but it's happening and I can't stop it." I still didn't really know what she meant, but I kind of thought I did?

"Does it have to do with the money or school or anything?" I asked. I needed to narrow this down so I could figure out how to talk to her about it so we could fix it.

She shook her head.

"No, it's *me*. I'm not explaining this right, but I don't know how to explain it." I was going to take a stab at this, and hopefully, some of my words would be right.

"People change, Care. We're supposed to as we get older. And sometimes we hide things deep down inside about ourselves because we're scared, or because we've been taught to be scared, and to lie to ourselves about who we are. Is that what you mean?"

She stared at me for a few seconds.

"Yes. I think so. I feel like I need to talk to someone."

"You can talk to me about anything, you know that." She gave me a sad smile.

"This time I think this is something I need to talk to a professional about. A therapist. I just... I need some help, Lo. I just need some help." Now I was going to cry, both because she was hurting, and because I couldn't do a fucking thing about it.

"Then you should. You do whatever you need to do, Care. I'm here for you and I'll support you. Always and forever. I just want you to be happy and safe and to know I love you." And there were the waterworks. I was all choked up and she was crying again.

"That means a lot. I wasn't sure how to tell you. I've been feeling this way since before everything happened and I feel like now that so many things are going on, I need to get this figured out before I go to school. I don't want to be distracted by anything when I'm trying to focus." That made complete sense.

"That's really smart. I'm proud of you, Care, for speaking up and realizing that you need some help. Everyone does at some point in their life, but not everyone is willing to say that they do. That takes a lot of courage." I reached for the box of tissues, pulling out one for myself and handing the box to Cara.

"Is it just me, or have we cried way more since we got married than in the years before? It's getting ridiculous at this point." We both laughed and blew our noses.

"It's like we turned on our emotional faucets and don't know how to turn them off. I hope I'm not constantly crying through school in the fall. I can't deal with that and exams." I didn't blame her. I was looking forward to having less emotional upheaval in my life. I wanted things to be boring and quiet. That sounded really nice.

I STARTED MY JOB THAT week, and I could tell I was really going to like it. Nothing stressful or hard, and I got to see all sorts of pretty art. Not too bad at all. I also met some of my coworkers and they were all ages and backgrounds, all sweet and helpful and interesting. No doubt I would get annoyed with them in a few months, but during training they were all ideal coworkers.

Cara called her doctor and got a referral to see a therapist. It still crushed me that I couldn't help her on my own, but I was glad she had found someone who could.

The purse came for her and she screamed when she opened it.

"Are you mad?" I asked as she hugged the purse to her chest and twirled around the room.

"What?" she said, humming a waltz and dancing with the bag.

"Never mind," I said, laughing. I think it was safe to say she loved the bag.

Our furniture came and the couch fit perfectly in our living room and ended up being just the right size. I had to admit, the other pieces that Cara had picked out really made the room look nice. Like two adults lived in it, and not just two broke college students who didn't know how to decorate. I even asked for her help with my room, and upgraded my twin bed at last. I splurged on a fancy mattress and I'd had no idea how much of a difference a good mattress could make. My back stopped randomly spasming the same week the mattress came in and I didn't think that was a coincidence.

We also got our wedding pictures back and decided to frame a few of them and set them on top of one of the shelves Cara had also ordered to decorate the living room. Our bouquets sat in vases beside the television. Just like a real married couple.

My parents called even more than they used to and spent half of their time chatting with Cara. They were taking this daughter-in-law thing seriously. I always rolled my eyes and handed the phone to her when they asked.

"They love you more than they love me," I pouted one night.

"They do not. They're just happy we're under the same roof. I feel like I should remind them that we aren't a couple, but I don't want to rain on their parade." I knew exactly how she felt. I'd given up on reminding my parents of that. They never listened.

Things were going fine with our friends, and I guess Cara and I got more comfortable with lying to them, which probably wasn't a good thing. Ansel hadn't brought up telling them the truth again, which was a relief. I did find him watching us with a critical eye every now and then and I could see the wheels turning in his head, as if he was trying to put something together. I wasn't sure what it meant, and I had too much going on to try and figure it out.

As far as the money situation, I told my friends that my parents had given me some money from my grandmother, and Cara told them she'd gotten a good financial aid package. They didn't seem to need more than that. It wasn't completely a lie. Cara's financial aid was good. The check had cleared and she was almost ready to sign up for classes for the fall semester. I was preparing for the house to be covered in medial books, and for Cara to basically go into hibernation and never see me again. Until then, I was going to take all the time I could with her.

We did almost everything together. I had lived in Boston for years, but I'd never done a lot of the silly things that tourists did when they came to town. We rode the duckboats and went to all the museums and galleries and even participated in a reenactment of the Boston Tea party by shoving boxes overboard from a boat.

There were whale watches and kayaking and walking the Freedom Trail and touring breweries. Cara got so enthusiastic and wanted to do anything and everything, and I was more than happy to go with her. Her enthusiasm was infectious, and she wasn't scared to look like a dork, even when one place required us to put on colonial mobcaps and churn butter. I'd never seen her so carefree, or seen her smile and laugh so much. I just wanted to be around that. Who wouldn't?

I also wondered if it had anything to do with her new therapist. After her first session, I'd asked her how it had gone and she'd said it was good, and didn't give me many other details. I didn't want to pry, so I didn't bug her about it, even though I was dying to know. I was trying not to be hurt that there were things that she couldn't talk to me about. And I sincerely hoped that the thing she couldn't talk to me about wasn't... me.

She hadn't said anything about annulment and I didn't bring it up. The very idea of undoing our marriage (even if it was fake) made me feel like I was going to throw up. I knew that annulling it wouldn't undo the ceremony we'd had or everything that had happened, but still. We'd done it and I didn't want to undo it. Yet. Not yet.

Eighteen

I came home from work one afternoon and found Cara and Ansel having what appeared to be a deep and serious conversation.

"What's up?" I asked, my heart dropping into my feet. Ansel plastered on a smile and got up.

"Just having a chat, and I'm on my way out. I have a hot date tonight." His smile turned from fake to genuine. I glanced at Cara who was also trying to smile.

"Oh, yeah? You think this is the one?" He burst out laughing.

"You know that I never got to have my casual dating days when I was younger, so I have to make up for lost time. I can see myself getting married. Maybe in ten years." I had the feeling if he met the right girl, he would be all in. We were similar that way. Once we met someone we liked, we stuck with them and that was it. Like when I'd met Cara. I looked at her and decided that she was going to be my best friend and here we are.

"Well, enjoy your casual date, and I demand full details afterward."

"Me too," Cara added. Ansel gave me a hug and a salute on his way out. I put my bag down by the door and sat on the couch with Cara.

"Do you want to order something for dinner? I don't really feel like cooking." She was quiet for a minute. Was I just supposed to pretend I hadn't walked into something?

"Yeah, sounds good. I'm fine with whatever you want." She got up and left the room, but I followed her.

"What were you talking about with Ansel?" I asked as I shut the door of her bedroom.

"Oh, nothing. Just regular stuff. Stressing about school." We both knew that wasn't what she'd been talking to Ansel about. Did I let it go, or poke at the wound in hopes that it would help?

I opened my mouth and closed it. I couldn't. I was the worst at this kind of stuff. I didn't do confrontation. Not that this was like calling someone out for being a dick, but I didn't want to hurt Cara. I didn't want to annoy or harass her. Maybe she had been talking to Ansel about me.

"Is it me?" I blurted out.

She turned around from where she'd been fiddling with things on her dresser.

"What?"

"Is it me? That you've been talking to your therapist about and were talking to Ansel about? Is that why you can't talk to me about it? Things have been a little weird, and I just need you to tell me it's not me." The words can out in a rush, as if from a broken faucet. I guess I'd been holding a lot in and I couldn't anymore.

Cara looked at me as if I'd hit her and then she shook her head.

"No, Loren, it's not you. It's me." I would have laughed if I had been in any kind of position to.

"Are you sure?" I needed confirmation. She nodded.

"It's all me," she said, giving me a sad smile.

"Okay," I said, but that wasn't really an answer. At least, it didn't feel like one. I was worried and confused.

I'd pushed too hard already, so I had to let it drop. I took a breath and started to back out of her room.

"Okay," I said again, opening the door so she could have her privacy.

"Loren," she said, and her brown eyes were full of anguish. A few tears glittered there as well. My heart twisted and I didn't know what to do.

"It's okay, Care. I promise. I just wanted to make sure." I left the room before she could say anything else and shut myself in my room for the rest of the night.

Everything had been going fine, but still, there was something going on.

I called my mom, because who else was I going to call?

"Something is up with Cara. Has she talked to you?" I asked.

"No, she hasn't. I did sense a little melancholy, or something else going on. She won't talk to you?" I didn't know if Cara had told my mom about the therapy, and I didn't want to be the one to share that with Mom if Cara wanted to keep it secret, so I told her that Cara was talking to Ansel, but she wouldn't, or couldn't, talk to me about it.

"I got all paranoid that she was angry at me, or regretting everything, or that she wanted to move out, or a hundred other things. I kind of attacked her and she said that it was something to do with her, but she wouldn't give me any other details. We've always been able to talk about absolutely anything, so I'm at a loss with what to do. Should I just leave her alone?" I was a mess. My best friend was going through something and I couldn't help her. It broke my fucking heart.

"Oh, sweetheart. I'm sorry that you're going through this. But I think the best thing you can do is back off and let her come to you. If you keep trying to get her to open up, she's going to close up even more. Give her time. I'm sure she'll come around, okay?" Doing nothing didn't feel like an option, but I guess that was what I was going to have to do. Nothing.

I hated doing nothing. It was like giving up. I would never give up on Cara, but I guess I had to let her come to me. Everything inside me screamed to run to her room, sit her down, and make her tell me everything over ice cream, but that wasn't going to work, and it might hurt Cara even more. The only thing worse than doing nothing, would be to cause her to not want to be my best friend anymore.

"Thanks, Mom." I hung up with her, not really feeling better, but at least I had sort of a plan. A nothing plan.

I couldn't sleep that night. Every time I closed my eyes, I imagined knocking on Cara's door and crawling into bed with her, holding her until she broke down and told me. But I couldn't. I had to wait, and the waiting was already killing me.

I didn't have to work the next day, which was a blessing, because I never really got to sleep. I just stayed up all night trying to read or watch something to distract my mind from Cara.

I heard her get up and leave the next morning, but she didn't say goodbye like she usually did when she left for work. We always said goodbye when one of us was leaving, even if it was just to walk up the street to get some coffee. Not today.

I lay in bed not wanting to get up or do anything. I stayed horizontal until my stomach and my bladder forced me to get up and take care of my body's needs, but then it was right back to bed. I forced myself to do some reading and made my way through a biography of Hillary Clinton. Thankfully it was more than interesting so, for a little while at least, I wasn't thinking about Cara. I finished the book and then I didn't know what to do next, so I put my hand in my pants and got a little busy. Nothing could take your mind off everything like a solid orgasm. Only problem was, Cara kept popping up there no matter what I did. I kept thinking about her hair and her face and her laugh, and even my fantasies of Cate Blanchett in a suit weren't distracting me from. Frustrated, I stopped and realized that I should probably get the fuck out of the house. Maybe a change of scenery would be a better distraction.

I put on my shabbiest pair of yoga pants and a tank top that said "I'M SORRY I'M LATE, I DIDN'T WANT TO COME" and my favorite pair of sandals. My hair went into the messiest of ponytails and then I was ready to go.

I put on my noise-cancelling headphones and started walking. We lived not far from a really nice park, so I made my way there, and it looked like I wasn't the only one who had that idea. I passed tons of people walking their dogs, and with babbling babies in strollers, and runners doing their thing.

I put on some loud and crashy music that made my eardrums hurt and set a brisk pace. I was exhausted as hell, but I was going to sleep tonight, even if I had to start running. Perish the thought.

After making three loops of the fairly large park, I sat down on a bench and stretched my legs out.

"Fucking fuck," I muttered to myself. "This is not working."

I went home and took a shower and went back to laying around until Cara came home. I sat up the second I heard the door open, waiting for her to come and find me.

She didn't.

My heart sunk and I crawled back under my covers, pulling them up to cover my face.

Then there was a knock at the door.

I sat up.

"Yeah?"

Good thing I hadn't been getting myself off. That would have been beyond awkward.

Cara poked her head in, as if she still wasn't sure if she was allowed in my room.

"Hey," she said, clamping her bottom lip between her teeth.

"Hey," I said, pushing the blankets down.

"Can we talk?" she asked.

"Yeah." I motioned for her to sit down on the bed. She immediately started messing with the edge of one of my blankets.

"I'm sorry about last night. And for not saying goodbye to you this morning. I'm just... Everything is so messed up in my head and I'm still trying to work it out. My therapist is helping a lot, really. She's amazing. I'm thinking about things in a different way now and once I have definitive answers and know what's going on, I'm going to tell you, Loren. I promise. I just need time." She shouldn't have to ask me for time. I should just be able to give it to her. I should know what she wanted, what she needed. I was her best friend; that was my job.

"You take all the time you need. Forever, if you need it. I'm sorry for bothering you. I guess I got too much in my head and got a little paranoid." I shook my head at myself.

"No, no. You deserve to know. You're the only person I want to talk about this with, but I just... I couldn't, and I can't tell you why. Soon. You'll know everything soon."

That would have to be enough.

"I missed you. I know it's only been like, a few hours, but I did miss you," I said, holding my arms out. She scooted over and hugged me, but let go quickly.

"I missed you. Even though we were under the same roof, it was like you were a million miles away. I didn't like that feeling at all, and I'd rather not go through it again. Ever."

"Same," I said. The ice had been broken, and we fell right back into how we'd always been, and I breathed a sigh of relief. I could deal with this. I could wait until she was ready. I could do the right thing for her.

ANSEL APPARENTLY HAD a great date because he would not shut up about the girl he'd met.

"She's just... so..." he sputtered and threw his hands up in the air.

"Wow, speechless Ansel. That's something I thought I would never see," I said. He and I were doing a friend date because he'd gotten out of work early.

"Honestly, I have never felt this way about someone. I'm trying not to get ahead of myself. I can't let my heart get broken. It's so fragile." He rubbed the left side of his chest over his heart.

"Poor Ansel," I said, rubbing his shoulder. He pouted. "But maybe it will work out. You never know."

"I mean, I'm convinced that everything good in my life will blow up in my face, so I'm going to try to think that way. Or at least hope that this won't be as bad as my last breakup." He didn't talk much about his ex, I didn't know her name, only that she'd wrecked him and had stomped on the pieces as she left.

"If things go well, I want to meet her. You know, give the stamp of approval. Plus, if she's as great as you say, I want to be friends with her."

"Maybe. We'll see." I had a good feeling about this girl. Firstly, she had a career as a mortician, did roller derby on the weekends, and spoke four languages and was learning two more. Seriously, who wouldn't want be friends with her? Hell, if she was into girls, I would want to date her. Sadly, she was not.

"And what about you? What are you going to do about dating now?" I started laughing because that was so far from my mind right now.

"I can't really date when I'm married to someone. I mean, I'm not polyamorous, and it would just be weird. Like 'oh, sorry, my best friend slash fake wife is calling, got to go' on a date." That sounded painfully awkward. No thank you.

"What about Cara? Is she also doing the no dating thing?" I had no idea. She hadn't talked about guys in a while, and hadn't dated one in at least a year. All her boyfriends had been short-lived, except for one she'd had our freshman year of college who had been pretty serious, but it turned out he had not only one other girl-friend, but two on the side, and Cara wasn't cool with that when he'd said they were exclusive. What a dick.

"I haven't asked," I said. The very idea of Cara dating made me want to throw up. Of course I wanted her to be happy and be with someone who treated her the way she should be treated, but I had a lot of doubt about any guys being good enough for her. There prob-ably weren't any that were good enough, and I was never going to change my mind. Still, if she found one that she fell in love with, I'd do my best to be supportive.

"Huh," he said.

"What does that mean?" I asked. He finished his drink and set down the empty glass, crunching on an ice cube.

"Nothing. Just making sounds with my mouth." I squinted at him in suspicion.

"Something you want to share with me, Ansel?" He shook his head and fished out another ice cube.

"No, Lo. Hey, can I ask you a question?" He was definitely trying to distract me and I went ahead and let him because I knew that if I tried to get whatever it was out of him, he'd snap shut like a clam shell and would refuse to talk. I'd been there before, and it wasn't fun.

His question ended up being about whether it was too early to get his new lady friend flowers, so we talked about dating and what a minefield it was. You never really knew what to do, and you always felt like you were doing it wrong, or you weren't doing it right.

"I'm almost relieved that I don't have to worry about dating right now. That shit is too much stress. I can't deal with that right now. Being fake married is enough work and stress as it is."

Nineteen

My parents had been begging for me and Cara to come visit them for the weekend, and Cara finally caved and said yes.

"You know we promised we would visit them," she said when I started to sputter my objections.

"I know, I know. You're right, you're right." I was being mean and ungrateful, and I did love my parents and enjoyed spending time with them. So we packed our bags and rented a car and headed out to the country for the weekend.

"I hope they're not planning to surprise us with a 'congrats you've been married for a month' party." I wouldn't put it past them after that whole reception my mom had pulled off.

"If they do, we're going to smile and thank them and have a good time. Right?" Cara said. She was driving and I was lounging in the passenger seat with my bare feet up on the dash.

"Right," I said, and sighed. "We should go to the Cape. Rent a cottage and play on the beach and eat too many lobster rolls." It was still new that we could afford to do things like that. I wasn't going to splurge and do it for weeks on end, but a little three-day trip would be nice. And we definitely needed to plan our getaway trip. We still hadn't decided on a destination, but we had narrowed it down to ten potential spots. That was huge progress, even if it didn't sound like it.

"We should do that before I start school, because after I start, I won't be going anywhere but to class, to the library, to the coffee shop, and home." She made a pouty face.

"I'll make sure we stock up on coffee and the good croissants so you don't have to go to the coffee shop too much, and then you can study at home. Just wear a hat with a sign on it that says STUDY-ING in huge letters and I'll know that I'm not supposed to talk to you." Cara laughed.

"You are very much underestimating your ability to be distract-ing." I made an offended noise.

"I am never distracting. How dare you." She changed lanes and then gave me a withering look.

"You are constantly distracting, Loren and you know it."

"I can *try* and be less distracting," I said.

"Sure," Cara said in a way that led me to believe that she didn't think that would work at all.

"Meanie," I shot at her.

"You love me," she fired back.

"Ugh, I do. I definitely do."

She grinned in victory.

"MY GIRLS!" MOM SAID the second we got out of the car. She'd run out of the house to hug us and help us carry our bags into the house.

"Wow, what a welcoming committee. You'd think that we've been away for years and not like, a few weeks," I said, and Mom ad-monished me with a 'Mom Look' as she put her arm around Cara and led her into the house. Dad was inside cooking lunch with veg-etables from his garden.

"Holy zucchini, Dad," I said, looking at the numerous green monsters that were stacked on the dining table.

"Your father went a little overboard with the garden this year. We're sending both of you back with bags of vegetables, so don't even argue."

"Why would I turn down free vegetables?" I asked, but Mom was ignoring me.

"How is the job going?" Dad said as he fiddled with things on the stove.

"Great, actually. It's not too stressful and the pay is pretty good. If I do well, I might be able to move up, which would be nice. I'm still considering getting a volunteer position, maybe at a library or an internship or something, since Cara is going to be so busy this fall and I don't feel like sitting around the house alone when she's in school." That didn't appeal to me at all. I'd rather be busy and missing her than being alone and bored and missing her.

"Good for you, Lo. I'm proud of you for not resting on the money. You could burn through that real fast if you let yourself." He handed me a spoon and I started stirring whatever was happening in the big pot on the right burner. Looked like my favorite vegetable soup with fresh gnocchi. Yum.

"I know. I'm trying to be responsible. My worst fear is that I'm going to wake up one day and that money is going to be gone and I'll be totally fucked." He glared at me for the language, but I ignored him.

"That's really smart. I feel like your mother and I have done something right. You're very sensible, Lo. I'm proud of you." He hugged me into his side and gave me a kiss on the top of my head.

Mom and Cara came back, both laughing at something.

"We're almost ready here," Dad said, turning off the electric grill he had going with sandwiches and zucchini on it.

"We'll set the table," Mom said, reaching for plates and then handing them to Cara.

"Uh, where?" I said, pointing to the dining table that had been taken over by mutant zucchini.

"We're eating outside," Mom said. I always forgot that my hometown was much cooler and less humid than being in the city.

Dad and I carried dinner out, and Mom even broke out a bottle of wine.

"You know you've been married for almost a month, so I thought we should celebrate," she said, handing me a glass full of a crisp white wine from a local vineyard.

I opened my mouth to argue with her, but it was useless.

Cara also accepted her glass without protest.

"To our brave and beautiful girls. We love you both," she said, raising her glass. We all clinked and drank and I gave Cara a look. She shrugged one shoulder as if to say "why not let them have their fun?"

I stuffed myself until I couldn't have another bite of grilled cheese and tomato sandwich, or another spoonful of the gnocchi vegetable soup.

"There's dessert, save room," Mom said as I set my spoon down.

"Too late." I put my hand on my stomach and groaned.

"Same," Cara said. "If you wanted us to save room, you wouldn't make such delicious food." Dad tried to hide a pleased smile. He was always a total dork whenever someone complimented his cooking abilities.

"Well, we can finish our wine and have dessert later, if that's what you want," Mom said, leaning back in her chair.

"Sounds like a good idea."

We sat and sipped and talked and I had to admit, it was nice to be here. I'd gotten used to the chaos of the city, and out here you could hear the sounds of the bullfrogs and the peepers and the birds. I'd been in the city too long. I needed to recharge.

Cara and I cleared the table and then brought out dessert, along with more wine. I figured if my parents were providing it, I was going to take advantage.

The cake was angel food with fresh strawberry compote and coconut whipped cream on top. I said I didn't have room, but I told my stomach that it was going to make room because I wasn't passing this up.

After dessert, we stumbled back to the house and Cara asked me if I wanted to go out to the barn.

"For old time's sake." I smiled and grabbed a blanket. The hayloft had never had any hay in it, but the wood was old and I didn't fancy either of us getting splinters in our asses. We climbed up the ladder and I spread the old blanket out before we sat down. Cara had pushed the doors open so we could have light and a fresh breeze.

"Wow, it's giving me major nostalgia being up here," Cara said, lying on her back. I joined her and looked at the bits of sunlight that had squeezed themselves through the cracks between the beams and holes in the roof.

"I know this place is falling apart and my parents need to repair it, but I don't know what it would be like if the roof didn't let in any light. It wouldn't be the same."

"I know," Cara murmured. "I always thought this place was so magical. Like it transported me to another place." We used to have a tire swing in here that hung from the ceiling, and we would take turns pushing each other and spinning until we almost threw up. The swing had broken years ago, but I was wishing that it was still working. I hadn't been on any kind of swing in years.

"Remember that night after the dance in junior high?" she said with a laugh.

"Oh, god, please let me forget." I wanted to bury my face under the blanket. "Why do you always bring up my embarrassing moments?"

She laughed.

"I don't know. I guess I don't think of them as embarrassing, they're just cute." I glared at her.

"That's because they didn't happen to *you*."

"Mmm, good point."

I closed my eyes and focused on my breathing. I could feel Cara doing the same next to me. I was getting into a totally zen place, when she sat up suddenly.

"What is it? Splinter in your back?"

Her face was serious.

"What is it Care?" I had been on the edge of my seat, waiting for her to confide in me. I'd never experienced so much anticipation in my life. Not even when I was waiting to see if I got into the college I wanted to go to.

"Nothing. Just... thinking." She rubbed her arms as if she was cold.

Moments ago she'd been laughing. This wasn't the first time she'd switched so fast and I was starting to get whiplash.

"Thinking about what?" I asked.

She pulled her knees up and rested her chin on them.

"Just life. The past. Growing up."

"That's a lot of things to think about at once." She glanced at me.

"Yeah, I know. Therapy has made me way too contemplative. Thinking about the past and seeing it through a different lens. It's confusing as all hell." Sounded like it.

"Anything I can do?" I tried not to sound too desperate.

"No, I'm good. Just being here with me and letting me blather on about nonsense is more than enough. And having patience with me while I figure my shit out." I could do both of those things. Not easily or well, but I could do them.

"Thanks, Care. You know I'd do anything. I've already figured out the best way to hide a body, should the need ever arise." Cara smiled and the tension in my chest eased a fraction.

"I don't even want to know."

"I'm going between burying it in an existing grave and dissolving it in drain cleaner and then grinding up the bones."

Cara made a face of disgust.

"You are so getting arrested for looking that up online."

"No way. There are millions of people looking up way worse shit."

We both shuddered imagining what those searches might look like.

"You wanna take a walk down the road?" My stomach was starting to feel better and I wanted to get up and move.

"Sure."

My parents lived down a dirt road that was off another smaller road where three cars driving down in an hour was considered "traffic." Gotta love rural New England.

Cara and I strolled leisurely, picking wildflowers along the way. My mom would love them just as much as she did when we were six and handed dirty bouquets to her with the roots hanging down.

"I can't believe we've been married for a month," she said, plucking a daisy.

"I know. It feels like it's been forever, but also only a day? It's weird how things can be like that." She nodded and shook some dirt from her flowers.

"Do you like it? Being married to me?" she asked.

"Yeah, I do." I was trying not to be too enthusiastic. I fucking loved being married to her. It was awesome. "And you?"

"It's pretty great." Cara gave me a brief smile. "So you're not thinking about annulment?"

"Not really," I said, which was a lie. I had been waiting for her to bring this up for weeks. We'd gotten the money, so there wasn't a logical reason for us to stay married anymore, but I still. I didn't want to annul anything.

"Oh," she said. "Then you think we should stay married?"

"I mean, there's no reason for us to. So I guess we can annul it." I could barely get the words out. They physically hurt to say out loud. Plus, they were lies.

"Yeah, we probably should." She plucked a black-eyed Susan and added it to her bouquet.

"But we don't have to. We can stay married. Unless that would throw a wrench in your dating life." It pained me to bring it up, but ever since Ansel had asked, I couldn't help thinking that she might want to start dating and not have to worry about confessing she had a fake wife waiting at home.

"Oh, no, I'm not thinking about dating anytime soon. Especially not with school starting. I wouldn't have the time. And I just don't feel like it." Something told me there was more to that story than just school.

"You're probably right. I don't picture a whole lot of guys willing to take a backseat to studying. I mean, I know there are, but they're a little hard to find sometimes."

"Mmm," she said in agreement.

"But you can date. If you want to. Obviously. You don't need my permission." I was babbling. I wanted her to be free to do what she wanted to do, but it would also crush me if she got into a relationship. The cognitive dissonance was real.

"I know," she said as we reached the end of the road and turned around. We had walked this so many times when we were kids we didn't even have to decide that we were going back. We both just knew.

"So you can. If you wanted to. Or not, if you don't want to." I cringed at myself. Why was I being awkward about this?

"Good to know. But I don't want to right now. Still figuring things out. And school too." I couldn't help but be relieved. So relieved I thought my legs were going to give out on me. I stumbled a bit and Cara reached out to steady me.

"Stupid rocks," I said, kicking a few away from my feet.

We got back to the house and went inside to play board games with my parents. It was one of my favorite things to do with them because they were both pretty mild-mannered most of the time, but something happened to them when the games were brought out. Things got vicious and hilarious at the same time.

We had more wine and did a lot of yelling and Cara kicked all our asses, first at Exploding Kittens, then at Life, and then at Jenga. She was on a roll.

"For the millionth time, I am NOT playing Cards Against Humanity with my parents," I said when Dad tried to get the box of cards out.

"There are some lines I will not cross, and that is one of them." He sighed and put the cards back.

"You can save that one for when you have parties with your friends. Not your daughter." I shuddered at the thought.

"I don't know, it could be fun," Cara said, and I aimed a kick at her under the table that she dodged.

"Don't you encourage them," I said, pointing my finger at her. She just gave me an innocent look.

"I'm being attacked," I said, crossing my arms. They all laughed in unison and Mom got up to put the games away.

"Well, in our old age, your father and I have started going to bed earlier. You're welcome to stay up as long as you want because you're grown adults, but we're probably going to head to bed." I raised my eyebrows at her. My parents didn't normally go to bed early, and I didn't think it had anything to do with being older, because they weren't even that old.

"Okayyyyy," I said, drawing the word out. "Well, goodnight." I hugged and kissed both of them, as did Cara.

Then it was just the two of us.

"You want to play cards?" Cara asked.

I yawned.

"Not really, but I'd watch a movie if you want." She agreed and we both grabbed blankets and got ourselves situated on my parent's couch. I was still full from dinner, but I couldn't do a movie without snacks, so I raided the pantry and brought out the fancy kettle chips and some caramel apple flavored popcorn.

"Drinks?" Cara asked, and I went back and pulled out a few sodas. We scanned for nearly an hour through all the available movies, and at last decided on one we'd seen about twenty times before.

Cara moved closer to me until our shoulders were touching and she pulled the edge of my blanket over her legs.

"You have your own blanket right there."

"But I like yours better. It's softer." I couldn't argue there; my blanket was better. My mom had found it and given it to me before I went to college, and it was one of the softest things I'd ever felt in my life. I'd gotten three more of the exact blanket that were back in the city at my apartment.

I swear, I was watching the movie, but I couldn't help glancing at Cara as she slowly popped one piece of popcorn in her mouth at a time. We should have picked a different movie that I had to pay my full attention to. This one couldn't hold my focus.

"Stop it," she said, not looking away from the screen.

"Stop what," I said.

"Stop staring at me. I can feel you. It's distracting." I glued my eyes to the screen.

"I wasn't staring."

She bumped my shoulder.

"Yeah, you were. Do I have something on my face?"

I shoved a handful of popcorn in my mouth, and then ended up choking on it and needing Cara to smack me on the back and several gulps of soda to clear everything out.

"You okay?" Cara asked. I gave her a thumbs-up and gathered up all the popcorn bits I'd coughed out and rolled them up in a paper towel.

"Sorry to make you choke. But you were staring, Loren." Yeah, I was, and I wish she would stop drawing my attention to it. Staring at Cara didn't mean anything.

I refused to answer her, so we just went back to the movie and finished it in silence. I was exhausted and wanted to go to bed, but didn't want to be the first one to throw in the towel.

"You want to just chill in your room for a while before we go to bed? I have a new book I really want to start," Cara said and that was fine with me. I'd been slacking on my reading lately and I was way behind on my reading goal for this year, in spite of having more time to read. How did that happen?

We cleaned the living room, putting everything back, and then headed up the stairs to my room. There were two guest rooms, but Cara always preferred to stay with me in my old room, and that was how it had always been.

"Are you sure you're okay with me staying in here?" she asked as I shut the door. I needed to change my clothes, but the idea of changing in front of Cara made my stomach do little flips of weirdness, so I grabbed the clothes from my bag and headed for my bathroom.

"Of course I'm okay with you staying here, what kind of question is that?" I left the door cracked a little so we could continue to talk as I was changing.

"I don't know, I guess I thought maybe that now we were older you might want to have your own space. And we are living together all the time I don't want you to get sick of me." I stopped pulling my shirt over my head.

"What the hell are you talking about, Care? I couldn't get sick of you if I tried. You're my best friend and if I could surgically attach myself to your hip so we would never be apart, I would do that." That made her giggle.

"It would be awfully hard to pee like that."

"We'd have to get like, adjoining toilets," I suggested and then finished getting dressed. She had changed too when I came back into the bedroom and I tossed my clothes back in my bag.

"That sounds really gross, no offense," Cara said.

"You're probably right. But the point is still made." She took her turn in the bathroom and brushed her teeth while I sat on the edge of the bathtub.

She blushed as she spit out her toothpaste.

"Stop staring at me, it's creepy," she said before rinsing her mouth out and then putting her toothbrush back in her travel bag.

I looked down. I couldn't stop making her uncomfortable tonight, I guess.

"Sorry," I mumbled.

Cara went back into the bedroom and pulled out a paperback from her bag. I followed her, not knowing what to say.

"It's okay, I guess. Just... it's a little intimidating sometimes." I sat on the bed and gave her a puzzled look.

"Why?"

"I don't know, let's just drop it, okay?" She buried her face in her book and that was the end of that. I sighed and got out my own book. The only sound for the next hour was the swish of Cara turning pages and the racket that the frogs were making in the pond just past the backyard. When I was a kid I used to bring a net and scoop up hundreds of gelatinous eggs and wait for them to hatch and grow legs and arms. Before they became fully grown frogs and salamanders and newts, I'd release them back into the pond. If I'd had it my way, I would have put a pond in the house and had a menagerie of amphibians, but my parents had squashed that idea. Someday I wanted to have a house with a pond in the back so I could sort of live out that dream.

Cara snuggled down in the bed and I realized that her eyes were drooping closed.

"Hey," I said, trying to take the book from her.

"Don't take my book," she said in a sleepy voice, blinking slowly.

"I'm not taking your book, Care, I'm saving you from dropping it on your face and getting the worst papercut ever." She made a grumpy noise, but let me take the book, making sure that I held her place.

"Where's your bookmark?" I asked, knowing that she had one. She handed it to me and I slid it into place and set the book on my nightstand.

"Let's go to sleep," I said.

She yawned so big I heard her jaw pop.

"Okay," she mumbled and snuggled further under the covers. I set my e-reader aside and turned the lights out.

"Goodnight, Care," I said, brushing the top of her head.

She mumbled something back that I figured was her saying goodnight as well.

I turned on my side, closed my eyes and waited for sleep to come.

Twenty

Sleep was elusive again. Every time I tried to share a bed with Cara, my sleep button malfunctioned. What was up with that? It was incredibly frustrating.

I tossed and turned, hoping I wouldn't wake Cara with my fussing. I couldn't find a position where my body was comfortable, no matter what. I kind of gave up on trying to sleep, hoping that I could trick my brain with reverse psychology.

I started trying to remember song lyrics from when I was young, which was one of my favorite things to do when I couldn't sleep. I was working on the lyrics to one particular song when I felt Cara wake up beside me.

I froze and tried to calm my breathing so she would think I was asleep. She made some noises and got up to use the bathroom. I calmed my face and willed my body to act like it was in sleep mode. I didn't know why I was pretending. What did it matter?

Cara came back and lay back down, sighing. I expected her to go right back to sleep, but I could feel her restless energy beside me. Now she was the one tossing and turning. I heard her softly swear.

"Are you awake?" she whispered, touching my shoulder. I cracked my eyes open.

"Sort of," I said, my voice rough.

"Can't sleep?" she asked. I shook my head.

"Me neither." She groaned.

"You were sleepy earlier," I said.

"I know, but now I'm not. My brain won't stop thinking about things."

I turned on my side to face her.

"What kind of things?"

She stared at the ceiling.

"I can't tell you."

Here we go again.

"Then I can't really help you, Cara." It was late, I was tired, and I couldn't sleep. My patience was wearing thin.

"Fine," she said, as if she'd come to some sort of decision.

Suddenly, both her hands were on my face and she was Right. There.

"What are you doing?" My brain skidded to a halt, and I couldn't even breathe.

"Showing you what I'm thinking about, since I can't find the right words."

I made some sputtering noises, like a car that wouldn't start. I still couldn't figure out what the fuck was going on.

Her face inched closer to mine and it finally clicked.

Was she going to kiss me?

"Tell me to stop and I will," she said, her lips so close that I could smell the toothpaste on her breath and feel the warmth from her skin.

I couldn't form the words. I didn't want Cara to kiss me. Right?

I shouldn't want my best friend, who was definitely heterosexual, to kiss me. Was this a fucking dream, because it was a confusing one.

I tried to open my mouth and tell her not to kiss me. The words wouldn't come. I couldn't say them. Mostly because they weren't true.

It was as if I'd been hit by a truck full of realizations and was drowning in them. I started shaking and Cara was none-too-steady.

"Tell me if you want me to stop," she said again, but I shook my head.

"What does that mean? That you want me to stop?" I shook my head again.

"You want me to..." she trailed off and I nodded. Once. She let out a shaky breath. Her fingers trembled on my cheeks.

I was strung so tight, I thought I might snap in two if she didn't do something right fucking now.

She stopped with her lips almost exactly pressed to mine. I could barely feel them and that pissed me off. If she was going to kiss me, she might as well kiss me. I didn't know why she was kissing me, or what it meant, but right now it didn't matter. All that mattered was her mouth touching mine.

I lunged forward, causing our noses to bump, but neither of us seemed to care. It was a clumsy kiss, a careless kiss. A nervous kiss.

It was also the best fucking kiss of my entire life. Hands down. Cara was slow to respond, and I almost stopped and pulled away, worried I'd done the wrong thing. She'd been the one to initiate, but maybe she'd changed her mind.

Doubts filled my mind and I started to panic, but that was when her fingers started stroking my cheeks and her lips responded to my haphazard kiss. Normally I had more skill and finesse, but this was not one of those times.

She sucked in a breath and kissed me back, pushing a little in a way that made me push back. We started to figure out a rhythm and how to fit our faces together and when to breathe. Her tongue was darting and tentative, as if this was the first time she'd ever kissed anyone. Distantly I realized that this was probably only the third time she had ever kissed a girl.

I pressed myself closer to her and finally let my hands touch her. I hadn't wanted to crowd her at first, but she was responding so well that I decided to give it a shot. I caressed her shoulders and then her arms, reaching to pull her closer. She made the cutest little sound of pleasure and ground her body into mine. My brain checked out and went on vacation and let my body take over. Every nerve exploded with fireworks where we touched. Her hands squeezed my hips, bringing me closer as she thrust against me again. I moaned and opened my mouth into hers, our tongues clashing together in a frenzy. Things were still a little frantic and sloppy, and only getting more so. I wanted more, so much more.

Her hands dug into my hips, probably leaving red marks behind. I wanted her to leave marks. I wanted to have a visual reminder that yes, this had actually happened and it wasn't a fever dream or a hallucination.

Cara reached for me with her tongue, diving so far into my mouth, I was afraid I might swallow her. Air was inconsequential at the moment. The only thing that I cared about was that she kept kissing me. I wanted Cara to kiss me forever. This could be my new full-time job. Just kissing her. I had plenty of money; I could support myself and give my life up to kissing her. That would be a life well-lived because kissing Cara was unlike any other experience I'd ever had in my life.

It wasn't just that she was my best friend. It wasn't just because I had apparently been waiting for this kiss for my whole life. It wasn't the way our bodies fit together, as if they'd been created to be with one another. It wasn't the little sounds she made and the way she kept trying to pull me closer and closer.

It was everything. She was everything to me, and always had been and somehow it took her kissing me to realize. And not even kissing me the first time. This was technically our third kiss. Not that I was counting.

Cara yanked at me and I almost laughed at how she was trying to pull me on top of her. I would rather have died than put on the brakes, but I was starting to gasp from the lack of oxygen in my pursuit of her lips. My eyes rolled back in my head and desire exploded in my veins as she tooth my bottom lip between her teeth and tugged at it. Why was that so fucking hot? To be fair, everything she was doing was hot. Her demanding hands, her impatient mouth, her noises of want.

I was utterly consumed by her and I didn't ever want this moment to stop. With trembling fingers, I started to slip under her shirt, being careful not to go too far in case I pushed her. I'd had sex with girls before; she hadn't (that I knew of, unless she'd been keeping the biggest fucking secret).

"Stop," she said into my mouth, and withdrew. I froze with my fingers just creeping under the hem of her tank top. Neither of us was wearing a bra, and her nipples were hard against mine.

"Okay," I said, my chest heaving with the effort of stopping. She was shaking all over.

"What is it, Care?" I said, brushing some of her hair back from her face. It was all over the place, and I was pretty sure I'd gotten some of it in my mouth earlier.

"I think I'm queer," she whispered so softly that I could barely hear her. The words still rocked me down to my foundation.

"What?" This wasn't possible. I knew Cara. I knew anything and everything about her. I would have known.

"I think I'm queer. I mean, I am about ninety percent sure. That's... that's what I've been talking to my therapist about." My body felt like it was falling, even though I was lying down.

"How long have you known?" This night had gone from surreal to completely dreamlike. Could this be happening?

"I'm not really sure. I suspected before the wedding. Probably for the past year. Then we got married and everything just kind of got weird and I didn't know what to do or how to talk to you about it. I don't know, I feel like the wedding just kind of was my catalyst." I was reeling.

"So, do you..." I trailed off, unsure of where I was even going with that sentence.

"I have feelings for you, Loren. Something that's different than friendship. Yes, that is still there, but there's more on top of that. I just... you're my everything." My breath caught in my chest and time completely stopped.

"Am I really awake? This isn't a hallucination?" That made her chuckle softly.

"No, you're awake. I didn't mean to kiss and drop this on you, but I've been thinking about it for weeks and wanting to tell you and talk to you and I just couldn't bring myself to say it. So I figured the best way to do it was to show you."

"Show, don't tell," I said, making a terrible joke.

"Pretty much," she said.

"So wait, can we back up for a second? This is all kind of happening at once and I want to make sure I've got this straight. Or not, I guess." Another bad joke.

"Do you want me to turn on the light?" Cara asked, but I shook my head.

"No, it's easier to do this in the dark for some reason." I didn't want the light to shatter everything that had just happened.

"Okay."

"So you, Cara Lynne Simms, are telling me that you are mostly likely queer, and you have more than friendship feelings for me. Did I get that right?" Even saying it out loud didn't make this situation feel more concrete and real.

"Yes, you got that right."

"Oh," I said, exhaling the syllable.

"Exactly. I know you probably need time to process and um, if you don't feel the same way, that's fine, I can figure my shit out and we'll get the annulment and I can move into student housing and —"

I cut her off with another kiss. Now it was my turn to say what I meant without words. I went right for the inside of her mouth and she opened immediately, as if she'd been waiting for me. Like we had never taken a pause.

I told her with my body what I couldn't articulate in words. Not yet anyway. I poured everything into this kiss, as if it was both the first and the last. I gave her my heart. All of it poured out until I had nothing left. That was the only way I could articulate my feelings for her. My show and my tell.

I ended my declaration with a few soft kisses, nuzzling her lips and nose.

"Does that answer your question about my feelings for you?"

Now Cara was speechless.

"You like me?" I burst out laughing.

"Yes, Cara, I *like* like you. A whole fucking hell of a lot. I have no idea when it started. Maybe I've always loved you, but I just never saw it. I told myself that what I felt for you was regular friendship. But ever since you moved in, things have just... escalated. I have been staring at you. And I can't stop thinking about you. Those vows I made to you, they were real. I pulled them from the depths of my soul. I meant it when I promised to be yours. I just didn't know, but now I do. I've known for weeks, but I've been in such deep denial. I don't know why. Maybe because you're too good to be true and I don't think I deserve you. I definitely don't deserve you."

Cara put her index finger on my lips.

"Stop that. I don't want to hear that you don't deserve me. Because you, Loren Alyssa, deserve the fucking world. I'm only sorry I can't give it to you. Who else would have given up thousands upon thousands of dollars to someone else without even thinking twice about it? You married me, Lo. You married me to help me live my dreams. Who else would have done that for me?"

"I needed the money too," I said, my voice muffled behind her finger.

"I know you did, but I also know that if you hadn't needed the money, you would have lied and said you did and married me anyway. You've given me the world, Loren. The entire fucking world." I put my arms around her, buried my head in her shoulder and started to cry. Guess the waterworks weren't letting up anytime soon.

"I can't believe this is happening," I said into her hair.

"I know. I didn't intend for this to happen tonight. I was going to plan everything out and make a grand declaration, or maybe be a little more rational and not kiss-attack you, but then it kind of happened."

"It did," I said, and I meant more than the kiss.

We held each other until we both fell asleep, my fingers in her hair.

Twenty-one

"Did you girls sleep well?" Mom asked when we went down for a late breakfast the next morning. Cara and I looked at each other and then away. If we stared too long, I would have burst out laughing.

"Uh huh," we both said in unison as Mom dished out slices of spinach quiche and roasted potatoes and bacon.

"Good, good," she said, distracted with getting breakfast on the table. Dad finally came back from the kitchen with a plate of toast.

"What is with all the food? This is enough to feed three families," I said, pointing my fork at the spread.

"Oh, we just wanted to make sure you were eating well," Mom said. "What's wrong with that?"

"Absolutely nothing," I said, shoving a forkful of potatoes into my mouth.

Cara kept sneaking her hand onto my leg under the table and causing me to drop my silverware, or choke on my tea or orange juice. I nudged her with my foot under the table and slipped her a look to cut it out because I couldn't eat under these conditions.

"What are your plans today?" Dad asked.

"I think we'll go to the nature preserve and get lunch at the café and then maybe ice cream?" I said, looking at Cara. That was our usual routine when we came back here. The city had nature, but nothing like the preserve where you couldn't hear any traffic or honking horns and could see more wildlife than just aggressive squirrels and birds.

"Sounds good to me," she said, folding her napkin and putting it on her plate. My parents were probably the only people in the world outside of a restaurant that still used paper napkins.

"You sure you don't want to hop on the tractor for me?" Dad said, a wicked gleam in his eye.

"That's gonna be a no from me," I said, and he laughed.

"I would also like to pass," Cara said, raising her hand.

"Why didn't I get any children who enjoyed machinery?" Dad said, shaking his head sadly. Mom patted him on the shoulder.

"Sorry, but that store closed a long time ago. No more children for us."

"Ew, gross. I don't need to hear about that, thank you," I said, cringing.

Mom just smirked and started to clear the table.

"WHY WERE YOU DOING that at the table? They could have seen," I said as soon as we were out of the house and into the safety of the rental car. This time I was driving.

"They weren't paying attention," Cara said, waving me off.

"I think you underestimate my parent's ability to pay attention to every freaking detail of everything." I turned the radio on low and found the local pop station, bopping my head along with the song that was playing.

Cara rolled the window down and gazed out.

"What are we going to tell everyone?" she said as I slowly bumped along my parent's driveway.

"Tell everyone about... us?" We still hadn't even hammered out those details. We'd passed out before that had been discussed.

"Yeah," she said, looking back at me and smiling, the air from the window whipping her hair around. Fuck, she was beautiful. So beautiful I almost drove into my parent's mailbox.

"I mean, what are we going to tell them? We didn't exactly talk definitions and moving forward and all that. Why am I the one saying this? You're the planner, Cara, this is freaking me out. I can't be the planner in this relationship." No way, no how.

She grinned.

"Being the planner isn't easy, is it?" she said, raising an eyebrow.

"No, it's horrible, make it stop." She burst out laughing and that made me laugh.

"But seriously, what is happening here because I need to know?" I said.

"Uh, what do you want to be happening here? Do you want to be together?"

"I thought I made that pretty clear last night." We had both made that clear last night. No gray area there.

"So you're going to be my... what? Girlfriend? Wife? Life partner?"

"Huh. Yeah. Technically you're my wife, but... I'm not sure if we should dive right into being married without the dating step in between. But we should probably still call each other wife and so forth around our friends. Ansel is going to lose his fucking mind."

"Yeah, I bet he is," Cara said. "He sort of knew that I was questioning. That's what we were talking about that day. I'm sorry I was so weird for so long. I just had no idea how to talk to you about this without telling you the other stuff." It had been a lot to take in all at once, but I had adjusted, mostly because it was as if everything in my entire life suddenly made sense. A peace had descended over me that I had never known. As if something had been out of place and had suddenly clunked right where it was supposed to be.

It seemed silly to say that all of this had happened to put Cara and I together. I was pretty sure some higher power hadn't arranged for my grandmother to die and leave me a bunch of money if I got married and then to make both Cara and I need said money at the same time after making us into best friends. There was no way.

Not that I wasn't thrilled that all this had worked out so perfectly. Tied up in a neat bow. Of course that wasn't how life worked, but at least this one thing had worked out for both of us. We'd have to figure everything else out on our own.

"I was paranoid that you hated me. Or that you wanted to stop living with me. That was why I asked you. I was so scared to lose you, Care. I'm still scared to lose you. It terrifies me." The only thing that compared to losing Cara would be losing my parents.

"Let's not think about that because I'm not going anywhere." She held up her left hand, her ring sparkling there. I hadn't taken mine off either.

"Agreed. But I have one question."

"What's that?" she asked, reaching for my hand. I clasped my fingers with hers.

"How do you date someone you're already married to?"

"No idea, but I have the feeling we're going to find out," she said, kissing the back of my hand.

"SO, THIS IS OUR FIRST date," I said, as I handed Cara her mint chocolate chip ice cream cone.

"Yeah, I guess it is," she said licking her cone. I was instantly distracted from anything else but what her tongue was doing to that ice cream cone.

"You look like you fell over and hit your head," she said, and I pretended as if I hadn't just been gawking at her openly.

"I kind of feel that way. You be careful with that tongue of yours." She grinned maliciously.

"Why, is it bothering you?" She stuck her tongue out and gave her cone a long lick.

"You are being obscene right now," I hissed, looking around to make sure no one else had seen the display.

Cara cackled and did it again.

"If you don't stop, I am going to... do something!" She gasped in shock.

"Oh, no, not something! Anything but something!" I glared at her.

"I am inches away from shoving this entire cone in your face, Cara Lynne. Provoke me at your own risk." I shoved my cone at her just to watch her recoil a little.

"Haha, that's what I thought," I said, going back to my ice cream cone, which was now dripping down my arm.

"You are ridiculous," Cara said in between licks. I was not going to stare at her tongue and remember how it felt licking the inside of my mouth. I was NOT.

"Yes, I am. And you're the one who married me, so what does that say about you?" She rolled her eyes.

"That I am a lover of the ridiculous," she said with a flourish of her hand.

"True enough," I said.

WE GOT BACK TO MY PARENT'S just in time for another lavish dinner.

"Dad, you really don't have to keep doing this," I said, as I loaded up on veggie and steak skewers cooked on the grill outside.

"It's nice to have more than one person to cook for. Well, two people, if I include myself," he said, wielding a spatula as if it was a sword. He was also wearing a ridiculous apron that had a crown on it and the words KING OF THE GRILL. My mom had gotten it for his birthday, along with the grill. If anyone else were here, I would have begged him to take it off.

"It's so nice having you girls here. Sometimes I wish you would both move back and stay with us, but I know that's not realistic. You're both adults, out on your own, doing your own thing. We just get lonely here sometimes." Ah, it was time for the Mom Guilt Trip. I had been waiting for this. Usually she did it on the first day and not the second. We were leaving tomorrow afternoon, so she had to get it in when she could.

"We'll visit more," Cara said, cutting of whatever I might have been about to say. She grabbed my hand and squeezed it under the table.

"Oh, you don't have to do that. We're not completely helpless without you. We have lives. I just like to see both of you so happy. Gives me hope for the future of the world." I shared a glance with Cara. Mom was really laying it on thick.

"We miss you too," I said, and Cara gave me a nod of approval.

"You're so sweet," Mom said, coming over and kissing me and Cara on the top of our heads. No matter how old we got, we would always be little girls to her. I guess it could be a whole lot worse.

"Dig in," Dad said, setting down his spatula. Finally.

"WE SHOULD TELL THEM," Cara said that night as we lay in bed together, our noses almost touching. We hadn't done much of anything beyond a few kisses since last night, and I didn't know if anything was going to happen tonight. Not that I would mind having another middle-of-the-night make-out session with Cara. That was the best possible way to spend my time. Who needed sleep? Kissing took priority.

"My parents?"

"Yeah. Before we leave."

"Do we have to? I really don't want to get into it with them and have to field questions. If you want to come out to them, I'll totally support you. They were great when I came out, so I'm pretty sure my mom would throw you another party complete with a parade."

"Yeah, she might. I don't know, I just think we should maybe do it all at once? Like a Band-Aid. Rip it right off." I gave her a look.

"Do you really think they would let us leave without making it into a whole huge thing that involved lots of crying and hugging and carrying on? I'm still coming to terms with all that's happened. Can we wait?" She thought about it for a few seconds.

"No, you're right. I'm sorry, I shouldn't push so hard. They might feel like my parents, but they are your parents and I wouldn't make you do anything you didn't want to." I knew that, which was one of the reasons why we clicked so well together. Mutual respect.

"Thanks. I promise we will tell them at some point. Let's just figure out what the fuck we're actually doing first. This is new territory for both of us. I haven't dated in a while and you haven't dated girls, oh, and we're already married. It's not like there are tons of other people in our situation that we can ask for advice from." She reached out and played with some of my hair.

"Isn't that the truth."

We stared at each other for a little while.

"This is so bizarre. I never thought, in a million years, that we would end up together. I put you in the 'friend' box and never even considered you as romance material. But so many things that I thought were 'best friend' things were actually romantic feelings that I told myself weren't. Dating girls is confusing as fuck," I said.

"Are you kidding me? Why do you think I've been tied up in knots for months? I couldn't separate friend feelings from romantic and other feelings. I kept asking myself 'do I feel this close to her because she's my best friend? Or is it something else?'"

We talked all night about little things that we'd brushed off in the past as just being "really close friends." It was so easy to do that, especially as girls. Even though I'd been out for a while and had had several girlfriends, even I lied to myself about what category my feelings for Cara fell into.

"But we're here now. And I think the timing is a little weird, but now if we want to get married again, we can just tell everyone we're going to renew our vows. They'll never know this wasn't for real. So that's a bonus?" she said.

"I mean, it's not the only bonus. Falling for your best friend is pretty fucking great." I snuggled closer to her and pressed my lips to hers.

"Oh, that reminds me," she said, pulling back. "I think we should try and take things slow. At least at first. I have no clue what I'm doing so you might have to be patient with me as I fumble through this. I looked some stuff up online." The lights were off, but I was pretty sure she was blushing.

"Oh, you did, did you? What kind of stuff?"

"You know. Naked stuff. I'd always sort of looked at it, but I always told myself I liked it because I could relate to their bodies? The lies we tell ourselves."

I moved my head so we were sharing a pillow.

"Did you ever like guys?" She hadn't exactly told me that she'd picked a label, and I would set myself on fire before I would demand that of her. Labels could be important and were so individual. She never had to pick one if she didn't want to.

"Honestly? I don't think so. It always felt *wrong*, you know? That I was faking it because I wanted to be like everyone else. I told myself that when I was nervous around them that that was what I was supposed to feel like. That the sick feeling in my stomach was butterflies, not repulsion. I'm still untying so many knots, Lo." I stroked her shoulder.

"It's not easy, and it's a process. Take your time. You don't have to decide right now." She puckered her lips for a kiss and I wanted to let myself sink into it and get lost, but she'd said she wanted to take it slow. I could totally do that, even though I had to pry myself away from her mouth.

"Thanks, Lo. That means a lot. Having you to help me through this is the best part of it. I want to figure myself out, to know myself. I can't help wanting to make a sexuality spreadsheet, but my therapist told me to just take my time, like you said." I laughed a little about the 'sexuality spreadsheet.' Only Cara would do something like that.

"As long as your sexuality includes me, that's all I need to know," I said.

"Oh, yes, it definitely includes you," Cara said, stroking my face. She had touched my face a thousand times before and in a thousand ways, but her touch was electric.

"How did I delude myself for so long?" I asked, and she pressed her forehead against mine and yawned.

"I don't know, because I was doing the same thing. All that matters is we're together now, and figuring out what we want our future to look like." Of course she had already thought about that. To be fair, she had had more time to think about this. I still hadn't had a week to process everything.

"You have spreadsheets already, don't you?" I asked, even though I already knew the answer.

"Yes, but they're romantic spreadsheets."

I didn't think spreadsheets could be romantic, but if anyone could make them, it was Cara.

"Bring on the romantic spreadsheets," I said through a yawn.

Twenty-two

"We're home," I said as we climbed the stairs to our apartment. "Wait, should we share a room now?" I set my stuff down with a loud thud. Even though we'd only been away for three days, I had somehow gone through so much laundry.

"I think we should wait on that, don't you think? If we want to spend the night together we can, but it would be good for us to have some separation? So we're not going from friendship immediately to marriage." Right. Slowing down.

"That makes sense." Even if I didn't like it. I was already thinking about how we could have the other bedroom as an office or library or whatever we wanted. It would be nice to have that extra space down the road.

"I'm not saying I don't want to. You have no idea how much I want to, Lo. The fact that we're not making out right now is killing me," she said, and I gaped at her. She was so cool and put together that I guess I just assumed this was easier for her than it was for me. What I'd forgotten was the part about Cara being a fabulous actress who could put on a front better than anyone I'd ever known.

"I'm glad to know I'm not the only one. Because if I hadn't agreed to this whole 'take it slow' thing, I would be tackling you right now." Fire crackled and sizzled between us and the room suddenly heated up by about several hundred degrees.

"We shouldn't be talking about this. Talking leads to doing," Cara said, even though she wouldn't stop staring me in a way that made it crystal clear what she wanted.

"Then stop looking at me like that."

"Like what?" she said, crossing her arms and smirking.

"Like you want to undress me using only your teeth." That made her chuckle.

"I think undressing you using my teeth would take far more effort than it was worth. Unless my teeth were razor sharp. Then it would be quite satisfying." At last she blinked and looked down at her bag. "But really, we should try and simmer it down."

"Good luck with that," I mumbled under my breath as she dragged her laundry to the back door so she could take it down to the laundry room in the basement.

It was a little easier to keep my hands off her at my parent's house, mostly because I didn't want to get caught. My mother had eagle eyes, and could spot any sort of change, no matter how hard you tried to hide it.

Here? It was just the two of us, no boundaries, other than the ones we set. If we chose, we could have sex for an entire week and never get dressed and no one would know. Sure, our friends might be suspicious and we would probably get fired from our jobs, but we wouldn't have my parents breaking down the door and giving us a lecture. Perish the thought.

I shuddered at the idea of my parents giving us a sex talk and followed Cara into the basement.

"I DON'T WANT TO WORK tomorrow," Cara moaned as we cooked a quick dinner of ravioli with a spinach, strawberry, and feta salad.

"Me neither," I said. We'd had so much happen this weekend and I still needed a few days to process all the shit that had gone down.

"I just want to stay here with you," she said, popping up on her toes to kiss my cheek. I froze for a second. I wasn't used to that kind of casual affection.

"Is that okay?" Cara asked as I tried to get myself together. It was a cheek kiss. No big deal. People in Europe did it all the fucking time.

"Absolutely. I'm still trying to get used to this new level of our relationship. Kissing wasn't exactly part of our established friendship." Cara rested her head on my shoulder.

"Except for that time when I kissed you at the wedding and then that time you kissed me while I was brushing my teeth. What was that, by the way? Were you just overcome by me sexily brushing my teeth? Do you have a toothpaste fetish?" I almost popped her on the head with my pasta spoon.

"No, I don't have a toothpaste fetish, Care. I don't know what came over me. I guess everything just built up until I couldn't help myself. I had kind of hoped that you forgot about it."

"No way, Lo. I don't forget about anything you do." I blushed and couldn't hide the grin that spread across my face and made my cheeks ache.

"You can't say things like that to me. It makes me all gooey inside."

"That makes me want to say them even more because you're so fucking cute when you blush, Loren." I hid my face with oven mitts.

"Stop it."

"Never," Cara whispered in my ear before she ripped the mittens away from me. "I have years and years of compliments to make up for, so be prepared to get showered with them. No, not showered. Drowned. I'm going to drown you in compliments."

"This is terrible," I said, trying to grab the oven mitts back from her so I could hide my red face.

"No, you're *wonderful*," Cara said, throwing the oven mitts to the other end of the kitchen.

"Oh my god, you have to stop!" I put my hands on my ears and started singing loudly.

"SO, CAN WE KISS GOODNIGHT at least?" I asked later that night when we were getting ready to go to bed. Now we were sharing the bathroom, even though it was a little bit of a tight squeeze. I didn't mind.

Cara spit out her toothpaste and rinsed out her mouth.

"Yeah, we can kiss goodnight. But no tongue, and no sneaking into my room for hanky panky." I almost choked on a glob of toothpaste before I coughed it out into the sink.

"Hanky panky? Seriously? Is that what you call it?" I hadn't heard anyone under the age of eighty use that phrase.

"You know what I mean," Cara said, glaring at me in the mirror. "You'd better not sneak into my room and crawl into bed with me and then seduce me." The idea of me seducing anyone was hilarious, and I definitely didn't think I was going to be seducing Cara. Her seducing me on the other hand...

"Why are you pointing the finger at me? Who's to say that you're not going to be the one who gets into bed with me and whispers sweet nothings into my ear?" While it was true I had more experience with girls, it wasn't like Cara was a shy virgin. This might be new, but sex was always a new experience with a different partner. A lot of the mechanics were the same. The key was finding out what they liked, and I could not wait to find out what set Cara off like a rocket. I had theories, but I wanted to know if I was right. I also wanted to discover all the little things that I didn't know about, that surprised me. Couldn't fucking wait.

"Because I have more self-control?" she said, twirling around and then leaving the bathroom, leaving me sputtering and indignant behind her.

"Who was the one who kissed me at the wedding? And who was the one who attacked me with her mouth at my parent's house like, two nights ago? Who was that again?" Cara paused in her doorway.

"Fine, that was me. But I'm much more mature now."

"More mature than two nights ago? I don't think so." We'd always had playful banter back and forth, as friends did, but now there was this extra flirty edge to everything and it made my heart race. This new dimension was intoxicating.

"I can keep it in my pants, Loren. Can you?" I gave her a defiant look.

"Are you trying to get me to challenge you to a bet?"

"No, that seems like a bad idea. I'm just curious which one of us is going to cave first." If the past month were any indication, she was going to cave first, which was a shocker. Cara didn't do anything impulsive. My spreadsheet queen.

"It's not going to be me," I said in a sing-sing voice.

"We'll see about that," she said, and then puckered her lips for a kiss. I took a moment to brace myself before I gave her the briefest of kisses. If I let myself have anything other than a peck, I wouldn't be able to stop.

"Goodnight," she said, leaning on the door.

"Goodnight." I gave her a little wave before walking across the house and heading into my room alone.

CARA DIDN'T SURPRISE me in the middle of the night, and I stayed up for a little while just to make sure. Also because I couldn't stop thinking about how easy it would be to go to her room and knock on the door. I had to press myself to the bed to keep myself still. The temptation was especially bad when I went to the bathroom because her door was right there. She was just on the other side, all warm and drowsy and beautiful.

No. I would be good. I would respect her wishes that we take things slow. It was only for a little while. At least I hoped so.

I CAME HOME AFTER CARA on Monday night, and I was completely exhausted from the weekend, and work had been a little rough for the first time. I'd had a woman who wanted a refund and wouldn't take no for an answer. Trying not to cry had been my main battle as she berated me. At last one of my coworkers, an older woman who was basically everyone's stand-in grandmother, had rescued me and had made the customer happy somehow.

When I walked into the house, I was met with the smell of lasagna. My mouth started to water instantly.

"Are you making lasagna?" I called out as I walked into the kitchen, dropping my bag in the hall.

"Yes, yes I am. Because I'm a good wife," Cara said, posing in front of the stove.

"What on earth are you wearing?" I asked, taking in the full picture. There was so much going on.

"Oh, this old thing?" she said lightly, twirling so that the skirt of her dress flared out perfectly. "You're too kind."

"And the apron?" Over the pink checkered dress that looked like it had been ripped from a vintage 1950s closet was a white apron, complete with shoulder frills.

"You look like a period piece," I said, walking around her to get the full effect.

"Why thank you," she said, dipping a little curtsy. I had no idea where she even learned how to do that. "I just wanted to feel like a wife, and I figured this was a good way to start. Plus, the skirt is awesome."

"I mean, this is one version of a wife before women had, you know, a lot of rights." She scowled at me.

"Don't rain on my vintage parade." I put my arms out and she hugged me.

"I'm sorry. I didn't mean to ruin your fun. You look gorgeous, really." The ensemble worked on her in a strange and perfect way.

"You should totally get a suit and then we could be an old-timey couple for Halloween." A tailored suit did have its appeal. I'd always wanted to try one.

"I think that's an excellent idea. You're on." Cara beamed and the timer went off.

"If you'll excuse me, I need to get dinner on the table, and here is your martini that is actually cheap wine." She handed me the drink and motioned to the tiny table we'd managed to squeeze into a corner of the kitchen with two chairs. It was already set with the nice plates, a vase with fresh flowers in it, and a few candles.

"This is fancy. What's the occasion?"

"Uh, it's Monday? And I felt like it since I got home early from work?" I nodded.

"Fair enough." She brought the lasagna out of the oven and I was so hungry that I almost started attacking the pan, but Cara slapped my hand with her spatula.

"It's hotter than the surface of the sun. I don't want you burning your mouth. Just wait a few minutes. I set a timer that will tell us when it's ready." She went back to dressing and tossing the salad and adding that to the table while I pouted at the lasagna and listened to my stomach growl.

"Is it time yet?" I whined less than a few minutes later.

"No. Just sit down and have some salad." At least there was that. I sat down and started to dish out salad onto my plate, but I didn't want to eat without her, so I left my fork on the table and folded my hands.

"I thought you were hungry?"

"I am, but I don't want to start eating before you, like an asshole. We eat dinner together in this family." Cara swooshed her skirts out and sat down across from me.

"Is that so? Are we a family?" I gave her a look.

"I mean, what makes you think we aren't a family? We're two people who live together, spend our time together, and love each other. Even if we weren't married, we'd still be a family." She set her elbow on the table and rested her chin in her hand.

"Huh, I guess you're right. I always think of the very traditional nuclear family, whatever that means. You know, mom, dad, and two kids." I made a face.

"I'm pretty sure that families unlike that have existed since the dawn of time and it doesn't make them any less traditional. I mean, look at how many guys in the bible had multiple wives. That's traditional right there." The timer went off.

"I don't think we need to follow that particular tradition."

"What, you wouldn't want to take more wives?" She reached for my plate and I got up to hand it to her as she cut a perfect slice of lasagna.

"I think, for me, one wife is more than enough, thanks," she said. "What about you?"

"I'm still getting used to one, so let's figure that out first and cross the 'other wife' bridge when we get there."

We sat down to dinner and I finally got to shove forkfuls of perfect lasagna into my face.

"Slow down, I don't want you to choke," Cara said.

"I'm hungry," I said, my voice muffled through a mouthful of food.

"You look like a chipmunk right now," she said, holding a paper towel out to me. I knew instinctively that I had sauce all over my face. Didn't matter. Food was more important than looking cute.

"Thank you," I said, swallowing and then gulping down some water.

"You're going to get a stomach ache. Seriously, slow down." I made a sound of protest, but I knew she was right. I always regretted eating this fast, but the regrets never seemed to stop me from doing it again. Food was just so good.

"Don't lecture me on my eating choices," I said, cutting smaller bites and slowing down.

"I'm your wife, I'm supposed to nag you about things like that. I read it in my new book." She got up from the table and dashed to her bedroom, coming back with a paperback. It was bright and cheerful and had a smiling woman on the front.

"You did not pay money for this," I said, wrinkling my nose at the title and then flipping through it. The book was a reprint of some "keep your husband happy" book from the 1950s. I guess it did go along with the whole theme, so there was that.

"I was going to go through and change all the references from 'husband' and 'man' to 'wife' and 'woman,' but it would have been too much work." She plucked the book from me and stroked the cover.

"Wow, that is... something else. The woman on the cover is so dead behind the eyes." I looked at her again and shuddered. Cara set the book down.

"I just read it for fun. I'm not sure yet what kind of wife I'm going to be." I wasn't either. I had only known that I wanted to be a real wife instead of a fake one for less than four days. Still adjusting.

"Well, I'll tell you what, I'm not going to be sitting here waiting for you to come home and have your slippers ready and dinner on the table and be wearing pearls and shit." Cara made a tutting noise, as if she was disappointed.

"If I can't have that, I don't know how this is going to work out," she said.

"Damn. We had a good run. I guess it's over." I went to get up from the table, but Cara snagged my arm.

"No, don't leave me!" She yanked until I was falling into her lap.

"This is an interesting development," I said, raising my eyebrows. "Was this your plan all along?" She gave me a sly grin.

"Maybe, maybe not. Can I have a kiss?" I granted her one sweet, soft kiss when all I wanted was something a little harder, a little rougher. A little more demanding. Sweet kisses were great, but I was in the mood for something a little different right now. If I shifted my legs, I could so easily straddle her lap.

"Don't think the thoughts you're thinking," Cara said, tapping me on the arm.

"What thoughts?" I asked, feigning innocence.

"You know which ones. The dirty ones." I wiggled a little on her lap and she let out a tortured sound.

"Why are you doing this to me?"

"Uh, because I can?" I said, but I got up so I didn't push things further. That heat was back and if she didn't want me to go for it, I was going to have to go sit in my seat and finish the rest of my dinner.

Cara took a few deep breaths and smoothed her dress, as if she was trying to settle herself down.

"This hasn't been easy, Care. How much longer are we going to do this staying away from each other thing? Because I might die."

"You're not going to die and neither am I. We just need to... give each other space. And realize that we are grown adults and are not sex fiends." I pouted.

"But I want to be a sex fiend. That sounds awesome. Wouldn't that be awesome?" She groaned again.

"Stop talking about sex, please." I was about to say something else, but my phone buzzed with a text. I pulled it up and it was a picture with Ansel and his totally goth girlfriend. Yes, they had declared their intentions. Cara was also on her phone because Ansel had sent the picture through our ongoing group text chat.

"Someone is falling in love," I said, replying and telling him how happy he looked and how cute his girlfriend is.

"She's kind of hot. I think?" Cara squinted at the picture, moving her phone around. "I'm still trying to figure out what kind of girls I think are hot."

I set my phone down and stared at her.

"I better be one of those girls you think is hot or this is going to get real awkward." She looked up from her phone.

"Oh, yeah! Of course you are. You're the hottest." It was impossible for me not to blush when she gave me compliments, even if I asked for them.

"I think you're hot too, Care. Like, off the charts hot. You should come with a warning label. You'd melt the polar ice caps." She bit back a smile.

"You know those ice caps are already melting, right?"

"You're so hot you could plunge our planet into a heatwave the likes of which this planet has ever seen," I said. Boom, compliment.

"You're hopeless," Cara said, fiddling with the last of her salad. We both finished dinner and then I took a shower. I didn't bother to put clothes on in the bathroom and just walked out with my towel wrapped around me.

I had to pass Cara in the living room to get to my bedroom, and she was reading another book. Thankfully it wasn't the horrible one from the 50s.

Her eyes flicked up from the page and then went back down to her book, but I swore her face was starting to get red.

"What?" I said, pausing in my doorway.

"What? Nothing," she said, staring so hard at her book, it was like she was using telekinesis to try and set it on fire.

"Uh huh," I said, opening my door. I could feel her eyes on my back. Once I was inside, I rested against the door and took a deep breath. Taking things slow with Cara was requiring much more effort than I ever thought. My skin was itchy and tight, and there was restlessness in me that meant I couldn't sit still, or focus on anything for long. I kept constantly getting distracted. It had barely been a few days and I was already a wreck.

"You've got this," I told myself as my towel slid to the floor and I stood there naked, my hair dripping down my back. It was too hot. I couldn't even put clothes on. I was also horny as fucking fuck. Had been for days, but I'd resisted taking care of it because I thought if I started, I wouldn't be able to stop and then people would start to worry that I wouldn't leave my room for three days and I'd blown all the fuses from too much vibrator use.

I laid my towel out on the bed to protect my pillows from my damp from hair and decided I was wound too tight and needed to find some kind of release. I also really wanted to sleep tonight.

I closed my eyes and slowed my breathing, which wasn't really happening. I was already so close to the edge that it wasn't going to take much.

Licking my palm, I slicked my hand down my chest, pausing to pinch my nipples just a little. A rush of heat went right between my legs and I arched my back. Fuck, I was beyond close already. I let my mind wander, and it went immediately to Cara, only this time I wasn't going to stop it. I was going to let myself have this.

My fingers made a quick trip down to my thighs, scraping the inside of them with my nails enough to make me shiver and for my skin to break out in goosebumps. I spread my legs open and added my second hand, stroking through the patch of hair that I kept short, but not totally shaved. Usually I took my time and teased, drawing everything out for a more powerful orgasm, but tonight, I needed to get in and get out and get it done.

I wet my index and middle fingers in my mouth and slid them inside without much further ado. A loud moan erupted from my lips and I hoped Cara couldn't hear me in the living room.

I curled my fingers, just stroking my g-spot before pulling out and thrusting them in again, using the palm of my hand to put pressure on my clit. This wasn't my first rodeo.

Another moan left my mouth and I bit my lip to try and be quiet. I panted and drove my hips into my hand, my legs shaking so hard they were making the entire bed tremble.

I was so fucking close, and then I heard a sound that had nothing to do with being in the throes of an orgasm.

A knock at the door.

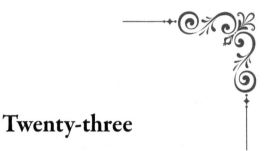

Twenty-three

I removed my hand and sat up.

"Yeah?" I said, sounding distinctly out of breath.

"Are you..." she trailed off, but we both knew that she had heard me, and what she was asking.

"Uh, yeah. I am." Why deny it? I wasn't ashamed.

"Oh," she said and then there was silence. I assumed she'd walked away, but then I heard her voice again.

"I'll... leave you alone."

"Okay?" I said. "You want to give me a hand?" I figured it couldn't hurt to ask.

"No, no. That's okay. I'm fine. It's fine. Go ahead. Fine, fine." I lost track of how many times she said the word "fine." Wow. She was totally flustered and that would have amused me more if my labia weren't engorged and aching so much that I thought I was going to die.

"Okay," I said again and then listened as she shuffled off, hopefully to her room to put in some headphones. I was going to try to be quieter, but I couldn't make any promises.

I let myself have a few seconds to get back to it, and then it was only a matter of a few careful finger-thrusts, a little clit action, and then I was flying high. I knew I made a lot of noise when I came, and there wasn't really a whole lot I could do about that, so I just went with it.

I gave myself a little rest before going for round two, and then round three. My hand started cramping, and I considered getting out my vibrator, but didn't want to go overboard, so I left it at three, even though my body was still aching for more. That would have to do for tonight. I got up and put on my pajamas, relishing the sensitivity of my post-orgasm skin.

I threw my towel in the hamper and went to the bathroom to brush my hair and teeth. Cara was shut in her room and I didn't think I was going to see her for the rest of the night, so I finished and went back to my room to read for a while, semi-waiting for a knock at the door.

My eyes started to droop after a little while, since I still needed to catch up on my sleep, so I got up to say goodnight to Cara. I wasn't going to break that rule just because she'd caught me masturbating.

I knocked as well and heard her get up and come to the door. She cracked it open a fraction.

"What is it?" she said, sounding irritated.

"Uh, I'm going to bed? Goodnight?" Her face was red and I could tell that she was thinking about it.

"Sorry about that. I didn't mean for you to hear me."

"It's fine," she said through gritted teeth.

"Clearly, it's not. Do you want to talk about it?" She shook her head violently.

"Okay then. I'm going to go to bed now. Goodnight." I tried to keep my voice light, but Cara wasn't having it.

"Goodnight," she snapped and shut the door. It was almost funny, and I chuckled to myself as I went back to my room.

I HADN'T BEEN ASLEEP for long when my door opened.

"Are you awake?" Cara asked, and I was suddenly very awake.

"Kind of," I said, sitting up. "What can I help you with?"

"You... Just..." She made huffing noises and then dove onto my bed.

"What the hell!" I yelled as she landed on top of me.

"How dare you," she said before her mouth was on mine and I stopped asking questions. My body knew what was happening and was raring and ready to go again. Like it had been waiting for this moment.

Her mouth was relentless, and it was what I'd been wanting all along. Her hands weren't sitting idly by either, they were ripping the covers aside, and searching for a way to get to my skin. I was just as eager, and in our haste, we weren't getting anywhere.

"Stop, hold on. We don't have to do everything at once," I said, as she kept kissing me through the words. She acted as if she didn't hear me, tugging at my tank top, and I was afraid she was going to shred it to pieces. My eager girl.

"Care, hold on," I said, trying again. She pulled back and I couldn't really see her, so I turned my lamp on. I had no idea how people fucked in the dark.

"I don't want to hold on. I can't stop thinking about the sounds you were making and what you were doing earlier and I can't fucking stand that you're not naked right now. Get these off." She yanked at my clothes and I almost laughed, but I was just as eager to get her clothes off. This wasn't going to be sweet and gentle. We were too frantic.

"Fine, fine," I said, yanking my shirt off, but before she could attack me again, I started to pull her shirt over her head.

"Bless you for not sleeping with a bra on," I said as I revealed her. "Fuck, you look good enough to eat. Maybe I will." I growled and ran my hands down her breasts.

She arched into my hands and threw her head back.

"Pants off now. Or shorts. Whatever. Naked now," she said, her eyes rolling back in her head.

"You need to get off me for that," I said, and she flopped beside me. I used the freedom to push all the blankets off the bed so we wouldn't have to deal with them.

"Give me a hand?" I said, smiling at her and wiggling my hips. Her hands shook as she pulled both my shorts and my underwear down my legs and threw them onto the floor.

"I've never wanted anyone like I want you right now. I didn't know desire could feel like this. If the world ended right now, I wouldn't care, because I'm here with you and you're naked and holy shit, your body is fucking amazing." Her eyes were wide and the only word I could use to describe her expression was awe.

"How have I seen you so many times before and never saw you like this? How?" I looked up at her and suppressed the urge to cover myself up. No one had ever really looked at me quite like this. Plus, this was *Cara*. This was the person I cared about most in the entire world. To be stripped bare before her made me feel completely and totally...

Naked.

I'd never been more exposed in my entire life.

"I want to find out how all of your skin tastes, and which spots drive you wild, but I don't think I have the time right now. I just..."

She looked me up and down and ran her hands up and down the tops of my thighs.

"Can you take off your shorts first? Please?" She struggled a little to kick them off, but at last we were both clothesless and I couldn't be happier.

"I don't even know what I'm doing and I don't care." I didn't care either. She could literally sit there and just poke me with her nails and I would be screaming "oh yes!" and "do it again!"

"Do whatever you want, Care. Experiment all you want. Put paperclips on my nipples, eat ice cream from my belly button, doesn't matter."

She let out a little nervous laugh.

"I don't think I'll do either of those things this time, but I'll add them to the list for next time." Right, the sex spreadsheet.

"You're not going to pull out the printed spreadsheet and cross things off are you?" I asked, half-joking and half serious.

"No, that would totally ruin the mood. I'll just do that after." Sure, just your average post-coital spreadsheet.

"Can we stop *talking* about doing things and *do* them? I'm going to explode." Even though I'd come three times earlier, being with Cara was on a whole other level. She only had to breathe on me and I would probably lose my fucking mind.

"Okay. I've got this." Cara was clearly nervous, so I sat up.

"I'm going to love all of it. And if I don't, I'll let you know. We'll get each other through this. And if you want to stop or take a break, just tell me. We've got this. You have a degree in biology, Care."

"You have a good point," she said, nuzzling my nose with hers. I locked eyes with hers and I could see the gears clicking and locking into place.

"I'm yours, Care. Only yours."

She put a hand on my chest and pushed me back on the bed and then straddled just above my knees. Not *quite* close enough for everything to line up. I tried not to pout, hoping she had a plan. What was I thinking? This was Cara. She had a plan for everything she'd ever done.

Except maybe falling in love with me.

"Such a beautiful girl," she said in a husky voice, running her fingers down my cheek and across my neck. I could feel my pulse jumping around, my heart beating out a frenetic rhythm.

I wanted to ask her if she was sure, but I also wanted to get off with her, so I clamped my mouth shut. This was her chance to do her thing and I was going to let her. Tonight was about her. It could be about me tomorrow.

Honestly, watching her decide how, exactly, she was going to have her way with me was the sexiest experience of my life. How was she so fucking perfect?

Her fingers trailed their way to my nipples, brushing over them with a tentative touch, and then stroking them a little harder until they rose up in little hard peaks.

"You can pinch them. Pretty hard," I said, figuring I could give her direction.

"Can I?" She raised one eyebrow, as if to challenge me.

"Try and find out." She wiggled her fingers and then slowly pinched my left nipple, digging her nails in just a little bit.

"Oh fuck," I said, arching into her hand.

"Interesting," she said, as if I was some sort of interesting experiment. Maybe I was.

Cara tried my nipple again and I knew I wasn't going to be coherent enough to give many more directions. The sensations of her touching my body were dizzying and overwhelming. And she'd only started.

She was going to ruin me. Ruin me or kill me. Or both.

Cara teased and tortured my nipples, getting the hang of things quick enough that she added her mouth, slicking her velvet tongue across my nipples that were so hard they could cut glass.

"I like the way you taste," she said. "It's... different." I emerged from the cloud of desire I was floating on.

"What do you mean, 'different'?"

"Just that your skin tastes different than anyone else's skin I've ever tasted. Better. So much better." Well, that was good. I let myself float upwards as she charted a course south, stopping briefly to tease my belly button and find out that I loved having a certain spot on my hips kissed. That made her smile and then attack that spot with her vicious tongue. I didn't need to give her direction, even had I been able to. She had me figured out so fast, I thought she might have taken lessons or something.

"Is it okay if I go down on you? I've been thinking and thinking about it and I want to try. If that's okay." I loved that she asked. She'd scooted down so her chin was hovering right above me. My legs had started to tremble with the anticipation of being touched.

"Yeah, you can. I love it." It was one of my favorite activities. You didn't necessarily have to have a ton of skill, just enthusiasm and the ability to get your fingers in on the action.

"Here goes," she said, looking down at me. I almost said something, but then let her take her time. It was cute and sexy at the same time. Made me remember the first awkward fumbles with my first girlfriend. They had definitely been more than fumbles. I probably shouldn't think about that right now.

Fortunately, Cara distracted me by running her hand across my clit and my thighs and almost down to my ass. She definitely wasn't wasting any time.

"Jesus," I said, my legs twisting and thrashing.

"Not exactly," Cara said under her breath and I was so beyond thinking that I didn't get the joke.

Her hands continued to stroke me, just barely, as she kissed from below my belly button all the way through the little patch of hair that was longer than I'd like (but she didn't comment on) and down, down, down.

The first little kiss from her lips on my clit had me jackknifing off the bed and almost taking her out with my pelvis.

"Down, girl," she said, putting one hand on my hip to press me onto the bed. I didn't exactly have control of my body right now. She held all of my strings in her hands.

Cara grew more confident, adding kisses all up and down, followed by little licks and then suckling against my skin until I thought my skull was going to turn itself inside out.

Her clever fingers were relentless, adding another layer of sensation that made stars explode behind my eyelids.

She popped one finger into her mouth, got it damp, and then slowly slid it inside me. I was about to tell her what to do to find the right spot, but she gave me the most wicked smile and then caressed the very spot.

"I took anatomy, Loren," she said, and I was too completely undone to care. I didn't even know what words were anymore. I could barely make sounds.

She flicked my clit with her tongue at the same time she stroked me inside and I had the most life-shattering orgasm. The waves started small, just ripples, spreading outward until they got bigger and bigger, great swells that shocked and consumed me. I couldn't breathe. I couldn't think. I could only ride and hope that I came out in one piece and didn't lose myself in the process.

As I came down, I was aware of so many little things at once: Cara, resting her head on the inside of my thigh, a contented smile on her face. The sound of my own breathing. The way the light caught the slight reddish tints in Cara's hair. The sheen of moisture on her lips, from me.

"Are you sure that's the first time you've done that?" Cara smiled slowly and then licked her lips.

"I told you, I took anatomy. And it doesn't hurt that I'm working with the same equipment. And I pay attention." She did at that.

"You're..." I couldn't find the right words. I patted her on the top of the head. "Yeah. Just, yeah."

"I'm glad you enjoyed it. Do you mind if I get myself off real quick? I'm so turned on I could fucking die."

I sat up and stared at her as if she had lost her mind.

"And what am I gonna do? Just lay here? I think the fuck not." I pulled my legs out from under her and then pushed her back on the bed where I'd been laying.

"No, I'm getting you off or dying in the attempt."

I did get her off. Twice.

Later on, when we were both wrapped around each other, I couldn't get the smile off my face, but I really didn't want to. We still had the lights on and neither of us had any intention of going to sleep, even though we were wrung out.

"Are you thinking about your spreadsheet right now?" I asked as she played with my hair, twisting pieces of it together.

"No. I'm just thinking about how you're all I've ever wanted and I can't believe I have you." I lifted my head from her chest so I could look at her.

"You have me? Is that so?"

"You know what I mean, Loren. Not that you belong to me, or you're my property, but that you're here in my arms and we're married. Who gets married and then falls in love?" I put my head back on her chest and listened to her heart. Every now and then our hearts would beat at the same time.

"Did we really fall in love after we got married? I feel like I've spent my entire life falling in love with you, Care. It feels like we're finally here, after the longest journey." She sighed happily and kissed the top of my head.

"You're right. We've been falling in love since you grabbed my hand and said 'you're my best friend now.' Bossy little thing."

I poked her stomach lightly.

"I just saw what I wanted and then spent the next eighteen years trying to get it. Some strategy." She snorted.

"You're not the only one who took her time. But we're here now. And I'm not going anywhere." Her stomach rumbled.

"Are you hungry? We should have some snacks before we go again." I sat up and looked down at her, spread out on my bed. The sexiest, prettiest, smartest, most caring, most compassionate girl in the entire world. *My* girl.

"Round two?" she asked, smiling slowly.

"Yeah, we have a shit ton of sex to make up for. I plan on making the most of it." I hopped out of bed and started to go for the fridge, but she reached out and grabbed my arm.

"The food can wait."

I squealed as she pulled me back into bed.

Epilogue

"So, wait. Let me get this right. You got married to get Lo's inheritance, you weren't in love, but then you realized you were in love and now you're renewing your vows after three months of marriage?" Ansel asked.

I looked at Cara, and she grinned at me.

"Exactly," I said.

"So you weren't together when you got married," Kell said. I knew it was going to take a while to explain this to everyone, but it finally felt like the right time. We'd called them all to our house and had promised Chinese food if they came.

"This is fucking wild," Cedar said. Jamie and Alex were speechless, and Jason wouldn't stop laughing.

"So you lied to us?" Anh said. I could tell she was hurt.

"We did, and we're sorry. At the time, I was afraid to tell you because we both thought that you might judge us. In hindsight, I realize that was a bad decision, and I can't do anything but tell you how sorry we both are, and that we will never, ever, do anything like this again." I mean, what were the chances that this particular situation would happen a second time? I didn't think they were high.

"Wow," Lane said. "I feel like it's going to take me a little bit to process this." The doorbell rang and I went down to get the food.

"Well, you can process with food," I said, holding up the bags. That broke the tension a little bit as everyone grabbed chopsticks and dug in.

"So what was the moment that you realized you loved each other?" Ansel asked. I set my lo mein on the coffee table.

"For me, I can't pinpoint one moment, but I feel like it really hit me at the wedding. The look on her face the whole day was just..." I trailed off and shrugged. "I knew when I was saying my vows that I meant every single word. I guess that's as close to a moment as you can get." I locked eyes with Cara and a tear trailed down her cheek.

"Oh, you're so cute I could die," Cedar said. "I'm not even a little bit jealous." Everyone laughed.

"And you, Cara?" Ansel asked.

"It was before that. It was when she had the idea in the first place. When she sat me down and said that she would do anything for me. And that was when I knew, and I spent the next few weeks lying to myself. Every other relationship had never felt like being with you. I always told myself that thinking about kissing you just meant we were super close friends."

"The denial was strong with both of us," I said and kissed her cheek.

"Does this mean that you're having another party?" Jason said. "Because the last one was great, but I think we can top it."

"Yes, we're going to have another party. Much bigger. Lo's mom is planning that one too." My mom had screamed when we'd told her. And then filled us in that she'd known all along.

"I knew you'd find each other in the end," she'd said. Dad had been all choked up as well, and offered to buy us a car for some reason. We turned him down.

Cara was due to start school in a month, and we wanted to do something to mark the change in our relationship, and what better than renewing our vows? They had been real the first time, but now we would both know that they were real, and so would everyone else. We were going to wear the same dresses, but do the ceremony somewhere else. We were still arguing about a venue. A honeymoon was also happening, at one of three locations. The list of potential destinations had gone down considerably, for which I was relieved.

Cara had moved her bed into my room, and a lot of her stuff. The spare room was currently a guest room, and Cara was going to set up a corner so she could do her homework and have some quiet time.

I didn't know if I had ever been this fucking happy. I couldn't believe my life right now. It was everything I'd ever wanted, but didn't know was standing right there in front of me.

"To Cara and Lo," Ansel said, raising his soda. Everyone else did the same.

"To Cara and Lo!"

I kissed her sweet and hard to the sounds of whistles and cheering.

"I love you in all the ways," she said.

"I love you in every way you can love another person. You're my everything, past, present, and future," I said. "You're my best friend, Care."

She kissed me again.

Acknowledgements: Wow, what I can say about this one? I have been obsessed with weddings FOREVER. Father of the Bride is one of my all-time favorite movies, and I've seen more episodes of Say Yes to the Dress than I would like to admit to. I never really thought about writing a wedding series, but then I figured "why the hell not?" There were plenty of non-queer wedding books out there, so why not take something that has been done and do it queer? That's pretty much my writing strategy at this point.

I'd been DYING to write a marriage of convenience book for... I don't know years, and then I finally said, "I'm doing it!" So here it is.

So many people have shown so much support to this cute little book. In this time of turmoil and terror, writing fluff feels like an act of resistance. I want to give you a place where you can relax and enjoy yourself for a little while. A world where everything turns out okay in the end, and there's lots of flirting and kissing.

My editor, Laura, is a freaking saint. She powered through this book on my extreme deadline and helped me make this book better. She always makes my books better and I wouldn't be the writer I am without her.

To my Patrons, especially Brandi, Elly, Ellen, and Amy. I can never put into words how you all keep me going, and have so much faith in me. When times are dark, your support gives me light.

To everyone on Twitter and Instagram and Facebook who have been excited about this book and the cover, THANK YOU. Sometimes it feels like I'm a lone wolf, puttering away on my computer and I have no idea if my book ideas are good, or that anyone will want to read them. You helped me power through when things got rough because I knew at least a few people wanted to read this.

To my Everything, I know this was rough. I know I had to ignore you and say "I can't do anything this weekend, I have to work," but you were a trooper and see? Now we can have fun THIS weekend. You inspire me and support me and love me even when I get crumbs on the bed, and that's all that matters. Thank you, love.

Author bio:

Chelsea M. Cameron is a New York Times/USA Today Best Selling author from Maine who now lives and works in Boston. She's a red velvet cake enthusiast, obsessive tea drinker, vegetarian, former cheerleader and world's worst video gamer. When not writing, she enjoys watching infomercials, singing in the car, tweeting (this one time, she was tweeted by Neil Gaiman) and playing fetch with her cat, Sassenach. She has a degree in journalism from the University of Maine, Orono that she promptly abandoned to write about the people in her own head. More often than not, these people turn out to be just as weird as she is.

Other books by Chelsea M. Cameron:
Nocturnal (The Noctalis Chronicles, Book One)
Nightmare (The Noctalis Chronicles, Book Two)
Neither (The Noctalis Chronicles, Book Three)
Neverend (The Noctalis Chronicles, Book Four)
Whisper (The Whisper Trilogy, Book One)
Deeper We Fall (Fall and Rise, Book One)

Faster We Burn (Fall and Rise, Book Two)
Together We Heal
My Favorite Mistake (My Favorite Mistake, Book One)
My Sweetest Escape (My Favorite Mistake, Book Two)
Our Favorite Days (My Favorite Mistake, Book Three)
Sweet Surrendering
Surrendering to Us
Dark Surrendering
Surrendering to Always
For Real (Rules of Love, Book One)
For Now (Rules of Love, Book Two)
Deep Surrendering
UnWritten
Behind Your Back
Back to Back
Bend Me, Break Me
Style (OTP Series, Book One)
Chord (OTP Series, Book Two)
Brooks (The Benson Brothers)
Second Kiss (The Violet Hill Series, Book One)
Double Exposure (The Violet Hill Series, Book Two)
Second Chance (The Violet Hill Series, Book Three)
Dirty Girl (The Hot Mess Series, Volume One)
Dirtier Girl (The Hot Mess Series, Volume Two)
Find Chelsea online:
Find Chelsea online:

chelseamcameron.com[1]
Twitter: @chel_c_cam[2]
Facebook: Chelsea M. Cameron (Official Author Page)[3]
Instagram: chelccam[4]
Sign up for her Patreon![5]

---

1. http://www.chelseamcameron.com

2. https://twitter.com/chel_c_cam

3. https://www.facebook.com/Chelsea-M-Cameron-Official-Author-
   Page-304422529610919/

4. https://www.instagram.com/chelccam/

5. https://t.co/mEdMCsdKxL

Marriage of Unconvenience is a work of fiction. Names, characters, places and incidents are either the product of the author's imagination or are use fictitiously. Any resemblance to actual persons, living or dead, events, business establishments or locales is entirely coincidental.

---

1. http://readheadediting.com

CPSIA information can be obtained
at www.ICGtesting.com
Printed in the USA
LVHW03s2300200918
590878LV00010B/325/P